ghosts of the southern tennessee valley

Georgene Mullins

ghosts of the southern tennessee valley

GEORGIANA KOTARSKI

*Georgiana
Kotarski*

JOHN F.
BLAIR
PUBLISHER

WINSTON-SALEM, NORTH CAROLINA

*The paper in this book meets the guidelines
for permanence and durability of the
Committee on Production Guidelines for
Book Longevity of the Council on Library Resources.*

COVER IMAGE
Chattanooga Area Convention & Visitors Bureau

All photos and illustrations were taken by the author unless otherwise noted.

Library of Congress Cataloging-in-Publication Data

Kotarski, Georgiana C., 1954-
  Ghosts of the southern Tennessee Valley / by Georgiana C. Kotarski.
      p.   cm.
  Includes bibliographical references.
  ISBN-13: 978-0-89587-326-2 (alk. paper)
  ISBN-10: 0-89587-326-5 (alk. paper)
  1. Ghosts—Tennessee. 2. Ghosts—Georgia. 3. Ghosts—Alabama. 4.
Haunted places—Tennessee. 5. Haunted places—Georgia. 6. Haunted
places—Alabama. I. Title.

  BF1472.U6K68 2006
  133.109768—dc22

                                    2006008823

Design by John Tarleton

To the memory of my father,
Ed Chitko (1925-2005),
who gently insisted I write a book

Contents

Tales from Southeast Tennessee

TALES FROM NORTHWEST GEORGIA

TALES FROM NORTH ALABAMA

PREFACE: ON BECOMING A GHOST WRITER

One night, I dreamed of ghosts, two genteel women dressed in white blouses and long, dark skirts of the late nineteenth century. They were politely and firmly intent on telling me something while I jotted down their comments on a notepad. But as is typical of dreams, I woke up without any recall of exactly what was said. The memory had faded along with the ghosts. However, I shared the dream with my husband, Dan, that morning, explaining to him that I was "interviewing ghosts." We both laughed and then forgot about it. For a while.

That June evening, I was surprised to hear an unfamiliar voice on the other end of the telephone. "This is Eileen Hoover," the voice said, "the new editor of *Chattanooga Life & Leisure.*"

I hadn't written for the magazine in a while. After our house had burned to the ground the year before, I'd spent most of my time rebuilding and refurnishing. My typewriter had gone up in flames. Without it, all writing had been put on hold indefinitely.

After we exchanged brief pleasantries, she asked if I would be interested in doing another piece for the magazine.

"Yes, I think I might be," I answered. "What did you have in mind?"

"Ghosts of Chattanooga," she said.

I couldn't respond.

She misread my stunned silence. "I know the lead time isn't very much," she said.

"Ghosts?" I asked. "Did you say ghosts?"

"Yes, for the October issue," she said hopefully. "We would like to use it as our cover story."

I didn't know a single ghost story, but Eileen had already run down a few sources for me. I agreed to turn in the story by August and hung up the phone.

"What's the matter with you?" my husband asked. "You look like you've been talking to ghosts again."

"Maybe I have," I replied. "An editor I don't even know just asked me to do a big article on Chattanooga ghosts. Of all the writers they have, she calls me. She's never even met me."

His lower jaw went slack. "If you hadn't already told me about that ghost dream last night, I wouldn't have believed it," he said.

I immediately set out to collect data on ghosts, knowing I had a short deadline. I could dig up stories and compile information, but I couldn't submit my work to the magazine without a typewriter or word processor to compose my tales. I still didn't have even a decent set of dishes after the fire. A typewriter seemed like a luxury. How could I have committed to this story?

Only days later, I attended the funeral of a dear relative. Another relative, on hearing that I had an opportunity to write but no typewriter, offered to give me his. He wasn't using it anymore and had been hoping to find a home for it. I felt invisible hands pushing me to complete the task. I imagined the two refined women beyond the veil feeling quite smug that I had been so neatly set up to do their bidding.

I graciously accepted the machine and set out on a ghost-hunting quest. I thought my mother might be a good person to help me get started. She lived in the 1925 white Foursquare on Bee Rock Road in Chattanooga Valley where she was born. Most of her family had died there, and the memories of caskets in the parlor haunted her still. Maybe that's why I had never heard her tell a single ghost story. But she is a great entertainer who can spin a tale as effortlessly as smoke curls up a chimney, so I asked her to tell me the ghost stories of her childhood.

"When the weather was stormy," she said, "the tree limbs would hit the side of the house and make a scraping sound against the walls. My granddaddy would always say, 'They're saying, *Shave me . . . Shhaavve me.*' "

I watched my mother carefully, eager to witness a creepy pantomime or hear of chilling disaster. But she didn't say anything else.

"Well, what happened next?" I asked impatiently.

"Oh, nothing," she said.

"I mean, what's the rest of the story?"

"That's it. That just always scared me to death."

So ended my first attempt at documenting a ghost story. I didn't think there was much character or plot development in that tale, so I moved on to the library in Chattanooga, where I found leads for several local legends.

I set out with a journalistic approach but often found myself being spooked not only by what I heard but also by who told me. The initiated were not hysterical, neurotic, or addled. They were generally educated, deliberate, and composed. Their very credibility was unnerving.

I turned in the article on time, and it came out in October 1989. In response, I was invited to appear on television and radio. One Halloween several years later, my stories were summarized in the *Chattanooga Times*. I quickly found that more people were intrigued by ghosts than I had imagined. Some of them came forward with their own yarns. Witnesses to ghostly happenings were not hard to find. Many people had experienced something they attributed to a ghost but were not inclined to talk about it until prompted. A folklore professor from the University of North Alabama wrote to me about the sentinel who haunted General Grant's headquarters on First

Street in Chattanooga. Some told me about personal encounters. Still others pointed the way to people who knew people who knew ghosts.

For the next thirteen years, I thought about expanding my research and authoring a book about local haunts. I sometimes hoped that someone else might do it and relieve me of my obligation. But by the fourteenth year, the spirit—or spirits—moved me, and I felt compelled to share the stories of these earthbound souls with a larger audience.

I don't know if the troubled spirits will now rest in peace. But I hope I will!

ACKNOWLEDGMENTS

A book does not spring forth from the imagination of one mind. It results from the experiences and insights of many souls. Readers will meet more than forty such souls—quoted as witnesses or named as sources—within the following thirty stories. But as in all prolonged labors of love, many people worked behind the scenes to move this book from idea to paper. I am grateful to them as well.

My husband, Dan Kotarski, logged hours and hours driving around the Tennessee Valley in search of the elusive. He waited contentedly in many libraries, listened to countless stories, walked through several cemeteries, toured three battlefields, read rough drafts over and over, and fiddled with various temperamental technical gadgets. My sister, Lynn Chitko Jewell, spent days making sure I met some of the most engaging ghost hosts in Chickamauga. Sheila Albritton Thompson, a ten-year-old boy in the body of a forty-one-year-old woman, went beyond offering her own story. She pushed the book forward with unbounded enthusiasm, even forcing me to visit the Chickamauga battlefield at midnight, against my better judgment.

Denis Kiely, assistant professor of English and folklore at Chattanooga State Technical Community College, answered numerous quirky questions about folklore and local history. Thanks are also due Hamilton County, Tennessee, historian Patrice Glass; Cleveland, Tennessee, city historian Bob George; Bledsoe County, Tennessee, historian Elizabeth Robnett; and the director of the Jackson County (Alabama) Heritage Center, Judi Weaver.

Librarians remain a writer's best friends. I met many good ones tracking ghost stories. Mary Helms, Jim Reece, Karen Myrick, April Fernandez, and Suzette Raney of the Chattanooga-Hamilton County Bicentennial Library pulled numerous files, maps, photos, and books on my behalf. Also quick to lend their expertise were Barbara Fagen, head librarian, and Elsie Brock, librarian, at the History Branch of the Cleveland (Tennessee) Public Library; Carolyn Walker, assistant librarian at the Chickamauga Public Library; Betty Johnson in Genealogical Services at the Cherokee Regional Library in LaFayette, Georgia; Vicky Leather, dean of Library Services, and Sandra Williford, reference librarian, at Chattanooga State Technical Community College; Steven Cox, head of Special Collections and University Archives at the University of Tennessee at Chattanooga's Lupton Library; and Carolyne Knight, head librarian at the Bledsoe County Library. Gratitude is also due the staff of the Sequatchie County (Tennessee) Public Library and the Scottsboro (Alabama) Public Library.

Book reviewer and bibliomaniac Karin Glendenning offered a credible, positive critique of my potential as an author, without which I might not have bothered to dust off my keyboard. Writers John Wilson, John Shearer, Chasity Brown, Cheryel Hutton, David Magee, and Vicki Rozema all tendered appreciated advice or encouragement.

Others who pitched in by reading rough drafts, answering questions, or putting me on the trail of sources included Linda K. Hixon, Frank "Bug" Shaw, Tony Bennett, Earlene Young, Lucette Brehm, Annette Reeves, Michelle Olson, Mirtha Jones, University of Tennessee at Chattanooga professors Roberto Rojas and Nick Honerkamp, Gail Shulimson, Mal Long, University of North Alabama English professor William Foster, Lynn Morse, Carly Thrower, Retha Earls Nelson, Richard and

Doreen Carr, Jim and Shirley Smith, Cathie White Rose, Sophie Hughes, Frieda Jennings, Jim Minor, Olivia Newton, Pamela Lane, Doc Bruce, Donald Tatum, Bradley Putnam, and Billie Baker of the Tax Assessor's Office in Walker County, Georgia.

The bravest among them—Sara Jewell, Forty-fourth United States Colored Troops drummer boy Steve Horton, and nurse-reenactor Kimberlee Bruce—posed for photos.

Ultimately, a book is only as good as its publisher. The folks at John F. Blair, especially editor in chief Steve Kirk, have taken the anxiety out of this, my first book. Having heard tales of editors more horrifying than any ghost story I know, it was a relief to discover an editor truly can be a friend and coach.

INTRODUCTION

Human beings have lived and died in the Tennessee Valley for thousands of years. As students of human nature and cultures have found, wherever there are people, there are tales of the restless dead. These stories are universal. Rare is the place that doesn't have a role in its mythology for those who have left the world of the living.

There exist enough stories in the lower Tennessee Valley to fill several books, but that does not solve the problem of digging them out of the nooks and crannies where they reside, often only in the memories of people who guard their reputations by holding such stories close. Convincing these people to reveal their secrets was crucial in researching *Ghosts of the Southern Tennessee Valley*. And finding one in every community proved unrealistic. Towns and communities not represented here might turn up in the next collection, if residents find the opportunity to come forward and share their ghost lore, realizing that such stories are part of our heritage and history, something to treasure, preserve, and enjoy.

The geographical area from which the stories were collected is large—a hilly green country traversed by a vast network of creeks flowing to the Tennessee River. Centered on Chattanooga, Tennessee, the area includes southeastern Tennessee, the northwestern corner of Georgia, and the northern tier of Alabama counties.

Home first to several Native American cultures before the arrival of the Cherokee people, the region was settled about two hundred years ago by Scots-Irish, English, and a smattering of other northern European descendants who entered the valley from the north and east. The wealthy among them brought African-American slaves with them.

Agriculture, coal, iron, and transportation by river and rail were the lifeblood of the region. Much of the economic development was destroyed during the War Between the States, which rolled over the area full force in 1863. The railroad that had once brought commerce became the coveted prize for Yankee troops hoping to strangle the South. Citizens were divided in their loyalties; brother fought brother and neighbor fought neighbor. Reconstruction was stressful but less so than for other states, thanks to Tennessee's many Union sympathizers. Still, decades later, the ghosts—figurative and literal—remain.

Nothing the scope of the Civil War seized the area again. But the small-scale dramas of life and death in the valley continued over the years through fires, floods, accidents, disease, and murders. Such is the stuff of ghost stories.

Scholars and librarians classify ghost stories as folklore. But the genre also crosses the line into parapsychology and local history, appealing to readers in all three camps. This collection leans heavily toward local history. Every effort has been made to ensure the accuracy of the historical information gleaned for the stories. But sources do not always agree. That is the nature of folklore and history alike. Sometimes, sources bordering on hearsay are all that is available on obscure topics.

The parapsychological aspects of these tales are not blunted. It is assumed the entities featured could be real and, as such, acting on motives common to human existence. Each story is viewed through a lens of compassion that questions the *why* of the haunting rather than the *how*, which is best left to investigators pursuing scientific documentation. Therefore, only cursory comments concerning quantifiable evidence are found within these pages. Many other books would be better choices for readers who want to investigate hauntings from a scientific angle.

This work touches lightly on the religious implications of some supernatural occurrences, but that is not its focus. It seeks neither to condone nor criticize a belief in ghosts but rather to document ghost lore for the entertainment of believers and nonbelievers alike.

The ideal story combines detailed eyewitness accounts with rich historical documentation that helps explain the haunting. But not all tales offer both in equal measure. Some consist almost entirely of personal descriptions of inexplicable events, sometimes told by people who asked that their names not be revealed. Others boast a colorful and exhaustive historical backdrop but few, if any, contemporary sightings or encounters with an entity.

Published ghost stories are occasionally criticized for being "told wrong." However, since such tales are spread by many people from many sources, it is hard to say which are the correct versions and which aren't. Correctness is often subjective. The correct tale might be the version most cited, the one cited earliest, the one that has appeared in print, or the one featured on television. Everyone who tells a tale, including this author, adds something to it—an impression, a likely historical connection, a new theory. I have noted variations in versions when known. But it is impossible to know all the variations. And even if it were possible, more versions would emerge in a few years.

In this collection, regular readers of ghost lore will recognize many of the motifs classified by folklorists. Motifs are story elements that turn up frequently in ghost stories regardless of geographic location. Common motifs include revengeful ghosts, headless wanderers, disembodied footsteps, crying ghosts, ghosts that replay violent deaths, hitchhiker ghosts, lost-child ghosts, and disembodied glowing eyes. Some of the encounters in this collection do not conform to familiar motifs. But then ghosts, like the people they once were, can't be expected to fit neatly into scholars' classifications.

tales from southeast tennessee

Murrell's headless corpse lies under a simple stone.

john a. murrell—
the headless outlaw

PIKEVILLE, TENNESSEE

*Ghost lore is replete with tales of headless apparitions.
Humans seem to have a deep and abiding fear of being
separated from their heads, and from such fear springs
many a creepy tale. Usually, no historical basis exists for
such legends. But the infamous outlaw who wanders among
the tombstones in Pikeville, Tennessee, is an exception.
He was robbed himself soon after burial—and it wasn't
gold or silver the burglars came for.*

A small black boy rambled through the pasture swinging a
stick at faded yellow clumps of broomsedge. The pale glow of
a new morning seeping over Walden's Ridge was not yet a
challenge to the light frost covering the rough grass. The boy
gingerly stepped around piles of cow manure, one still
steaming, and called out to the herd, placidly grazing beyond

Murrell's forlorn gravesite, front center, on a Bledsoe County hilltop.

a grove of cedars. About a hundred paces back, an old slave plodded along behind the boy like he did every morning, getting the cows up and bringing them in, after which he would milk each one, then turn them back out onto some of the most prosperous farmland in Tennessee, the bottom lands of the Sequatchie Valley.

The boy stopped walking, then dropped his stick, transfixed by a terrifying site on the hilltop. The infamous outlaw John A. Murrell had returned to life. Sitting up in his coffin over clotted, dark earth, Murrell appeared to have dug himself out. Now reanimated, he looked ready to rejoin the living, for what purpose the boy could only imagine.

The boy stumbled back a step, then turned and raced past the man. Across the rolling fields, he sailed over two split-rail fences, knocking one down, then splashed through the branch with his shoes still on, heading toward his master's home almost a mile away. The old man spied the horror, turned heel, and, regaining the speed of his youth, soon caught up with the boy. The two reached the house together. Alarm seized everyone in the John Billingsley household. They gathered around to try to calm the two and find out just what the trouble might be.

Having learned something was amiss at the cemetery, Squire Billingsley, the owner of the farm, the cemetery, and the slaves, rode up to investigate. It was indeed a morbid scene, even worse than the slaves had realized. Robbers had bashed in the coffin lid. Murrell had been exhumed, then crudely decapitated. His head was nowhere to be found. His body, left crosswise to the casket, had been partially devoured by hogs. Whoever had violated the sanctity of the grave had no scruples about leaving the corpse exposed.

Body snatchers were reviled in those days—1844, to be exact. After committing such a heinous crime, they would do well to escape with all haste. And these ghouls did. After stowing the bloody head in the back of a buggy, they had hightailed it over Rankin Branch and headed south toward Marion County, from whence they had come.

Other dead men lay peacefully in their graves throughout the quiet Sequatchie Valley that chill night. What kind of man was Murrell that his mortal remains would be hunted and mutilated, then tossed away like a chicken discarded by a weasel?

Many considered Murrell a diabolical genius. His life, from beginning to end, fascinated folks. For more than a decade, little children both black and white had been kept on the straight and narrow by their parents' threats that Murrell would eat them.

Scholars were not immune to speculation. "One almost imagines there may have been a smell of sulphur on his breath," wrote Paul Wellman. Murrell was known everywhere in the South as the most dangerous outlaw of his time. And he liked it that way.

John A. Murrell was born to a mother of calculating and deliberate evil. Zilpah Murrell, a demon of a woman, sashayed recklessly about her wayside tavern near Columbia, Tennessee, teaching her children the criminal arts while her husband traveled. Little John became her star pupil. He

5

admired her greatly. "My mother was of the pure grit; she learnt me and all her children how to steal as soon as we could walk. At ten years old, I was not a bad hand," he supposedly told his soon-to-be nemesis, Virgil Stewart.

His father was an itinerant preacher who embraced and emboldened evil in the time-honored tradition—by ignoring it. And so it grew within the boy until it took him. "My father was an honest man, I expect," Murrell said, according to Ross Phares, "and tried to raise me honest. But I think none the less of him for that."

Murrell was an accomplished thief by age twelve. He was arrested at least twice in his youth on minor charges such as gambling. He got into more trouble with the law when he robbed a peddler. At sixteen, he made his first raid, and his heart beat with joy. He knew he was cut out for banditry. Bolstered by his success and his mother's praise, he eagerly took to the roads and trails around his home in Williamson County, Tennessee, profit and fame on his mind.

His mother had instilled in him a hate for people of "quality," particularly Southerners and Westerners who practiced a dogmatic religion. This hatred shaped his life. There was not a fine horse or slave within his reach that he did not covet. And to sweeten the trap he set for those he despised, he styled himself as a gentleman to blend in with them. He robbed and conned at will.

Finally, the law forced him to face serious punishment for the theft of a black mare from a widow. Murrell appeared at his trial handsomely dressed and seemed the least concerned man there. Found guilty, he was sentenced to twelve months in jail, a flogging, and immediate branding with the letters *H. T.* for *Horse Thief.* In the courtroom, Murrell's hand was tied to the railing with a piece of new hemp. The sheriff, according to an account quoted by Emma Inman Williams, "took from the stove the branding iron, glanced at it, found it red hot, and put it on Murrell's thumb. The skin fried like meat. Horton held

"Murrell in Custody of the Regulators"
from *National Police Gazette*, January 23, 1947

the iron on Murrell's hand until the smoke rose two feet. Murrell stood the ordeal without flinching. When his hand was released he calmly tied a handkerchief around it and went back to the jail. Here he was to receive the lashes and go into the pillory, but the whipping was too much for his powers of endurance. Several times in compliance with Murrell's request sheriff Horton held his whip to give Murrell time to get his breath and collect his nerve for the blood-fetching blows to follow."

The brand was probably burned into the muscular area next to the thumb, known as the "brawn." This event turned Murrell from bad to sinister. The hurt to his pride burned deeper than the brand. He vowed war without mercy on his fellow man. Evil cuts deepest when it is gloved in seeming respectability. Murrell further honed his skills to serve more wicked ends.

He cut a dashing figure, according to Virgil Stewart. Murrell was tall, slender, and endowed with a "certain animal grace" of movement. His dark auburn hair fell long and curly around a fine face. His frosty blue eyes, judging by his womanizing reputation, had slain many of the fair sex. The qualities of his mind and spirit were those of a true hero, wrote Stewart, who called Murrell "a princely fellow . . . [a] noble leader . . . [a] wondrous man . . . who was unrivalled in mental powers . . . [and] universally loved by his friends." Murrell also possessed the gift of unflinching courage. Most disarming, he had an irresistible, childlike spontaneity about him. Yet, said biographer Robert Coates, "he had the flat pale glance of a killer."

Ever genteel and well spoken, Murrell was graciously received in homes, churches, and taverns "as a young gentleman of means and piety," said a 1945 *Bledsonian Banner* article. He could turn bitter enemies into admirers. Like the devil himself, he used his almost supernatural powers to seduce all manner of men. And women.

He took special delight in mocking true believers by posing as a preacher. His thorough knowledge of scripture served him—if not the Lord—well. A congregation would sit thunderstruck by his words of hellfire and damnation. Women clasped his hands in tearful gratitude, and children were drawn to him like filings to a magnet. And while he was bringing congregations to their knees with his soul-wrenching sermons, his men were outside stealing the horses. Brother Murrell easily passed counterfeit money in this disguise. For years, no one caught on. "I preached some d--- fine sermons," he later bragged, according to Nina Leftwich.

Murrell was rumored to operate over broad areas of the central South, including Tennessee, Arkansas, Mississippi, Louisiana, and Alabama. Unhampered by scruples, he robbed and murdered untold numbers of hapless travelers. He learned early that he could extend his influence and wealth by strategically appointing followers, each assigned to the area of his talent—stealing, killing, threatening, scouting, or fencing. Soon, his gang evolved into the Mystic Clan, a brotherhood similar in structure to the later Ku Klux Klan. One thousand men vowed to do Murrell's bidding through a blood oath and secret rituals. Many prominent men were rumored to attend the clandestine meetings. That explained, people whispered, why the clan could pillage at will and avoid the law. Terror gripped the middle South.

Despite Murrell's growing criminal empire, he maintained his aura of respectability. He built a fine rock house and installed a "Mrs. Murrell" within. It is unclear whether she was a good girl gone bad who really loved him or a lady of the amorous arts who functioned as his business partner.

His own vanity finally brought Murrell down. Virgil Stewart infiltrated the clan, intent on bringing Murrell in. He played to Murrell's self-importance while he pumped him for incriminating information and learned the whereabouts of the secret hideouts. He led the law straight to Murrell in Tennessee. Murrell was arrested but broke jail and fled to Florence, Alabama. His seventy-four-year-old father had posted bond on Murrell's promise to appear in court. Murrell broke that promise. Williamson County records from 1824 report that the Reverend Murrell's son had "always been an expense to him." The law recaptured Murrell in Alabama and returned him to Tennessee for trial.

Spectators packed the Jackson courthouse. His attorney—appointed for Murrell because he claimed poverty—was advised not to represent him for the sake of his career. But he did.

The traitor Stewart testified against Murrell for several hours. Murrell prided himself on thoroughness, said Stewart, killing victims to keep them quiet. He resold slaves several times, promising them their freedom if they cooperated, then killed them, gutted them, and threw them in the river. He had murdered one man near Crab Orchard, Tennessee, and rolled his body off the bluff. Stewart claimed that Murrell had also robbed a young man whose pockets were full of love letters rather than money. Taking what little the man had after he had killed him, Murrell said, "I thought all such fools ought to die as soon as possible." The most serious accusation was conspiracy to incite a slave revolt. While slaves and slaveholders were killing each other, Stewart said, Murrell planned to profit from the chaos by plundering.

When Murrell was first captured, many expected him to hang for murder. But despite enough evidence to execute a man several times over, the most infamous outlaw of the time was convicted only of slave stealing. The color drained from Murrell's face at the realization that he would spend years at hard labor in the penitentiary. Yet Murrell got off light. Over fifty white men and an unknown number of black men, mostly freedmen, were rounded up in the sting and were either hanged or brutally whipped and exiled, all based on Stewart's accusations.

Despite Stewart's success in orchestrating Murrell's downfall, he was not a popular man. Folks called him a traitor and an oath breaker and compared him to Judas. Many even in Murrell's stomping ground did not believe him guilty of heinous murder and widespread bedlam. Stewart was accused of fabricating his tales—which he published in a popular and profitable book—for revenge or simple greed. Scholarly research bears out this skepticism. Murrell was not convicted of murder, and there is no evidence besides Stewart's tales that he murdered anyone. Some even scoff at Murrell, calling him a second-rate petty thief or a coward.

Murrell entered prison in 1834, leaving two daughters, possibly a son, and his wife, Elizabeth, who finally divorced him and remarried soon thereafter. His many friends evaporated like dew under a harsh sun.

Life proved hard for John A. Murrell in prison. Fearing his gang might try to break him out, officials fitted him with a heavy ball and chain. He was treated like an ape in a zoo, often subjected to a barrage of curious visitors. "There was nothing else to do in Nashville at that time. The penitentiary was new—somewhere to go," explains Bledsoe County historian

"Murrell Escaping from the Bagnio"
from *National Police Gazette*, October 31, 1846

Elizabeth Robnett. Murrell met the stares of unwelcome visitors with the wary glare of a trapped animal. His pride was sorely wounded. In desperation, he attempted to escape by jumping off a brick wall and broke a leg. Shortly thereafter, he developed tuberculosis.

A well-known phrenologist, Professor O. S. Fowler, visited the prison and examined Murrell's head. Phrenologists theorized—incorrectly, it turns out—that a person's character and intelligence could be determined from skull shape. Murrell's bump of acquisitiveness was extraordinarily developed, the professor claimed, according to biographer H. R. Howard.

Even as a weak and powerless inmate, Murrell still possessed charisma. Prison records report his conduct as commendable. Carolyne Knight, Bledsoe County library director, says he was well liked at the prison and was sometimes allowed to go to Sulphur Springs in hopes of a cure.

Finally, due to Murrell's poor health, the governor pardoned him. He was released April 3, 1844, after serving almost ten years. On leaving, he admitted to most of the crimes charged against him, except murder. Murrell told the warden he was a poor man. When asked point-blank if he had any hidden treasure, he answered no. He did say he had come across a mine in the Cumberland Mountains during his travels, where he planned to go at once to financially replenish himself. He supposedly told people that when he had traveled through the Cumberlands earlier, he had left a bag of gold in the knothole of a tree, says Knight. "But then he never could find it again." Robnett says the prison physician directed Murrell to go immediately to the Cumberland Mountains, where he could be free from the noise and confusion of the prison workshop and regain his health in the favorable climate.

Murrell was considered an old man even though he was just thirty-eight or forty. He may have also had syphilis, Knight says, "because of his self-avowed lifestyle." Syphilis, incurable then, may be the reason some accounts describe him as an imbecile at the time of his release.

"He caught a stage to Sparta," says Robnett. "He may have had just a little money given to him by the prison."

"He comes across the mountain on foot carrying his belongings on his back," Knight says. "There, he met a man named Jack Mitchell at Braden's Knob near Fall Creek Falls. Mitchell was a blacksmith, so Murrell stopped and offered to do some work for him." Business was likely good, as the shop served a well-traveled road.

"He was an expert blacksmith," according to Robnett. "He could make plow points, it seemed. Iron plow points were something at this time, in the 1840s." Demand for Murrell's work was high. Murrell worked under the name of John Andrews, says Robnett. "He didn't announce who he was. Of course not! It wouldn't have been smart, would it? However, later it was found out. Scott Terry recognized him." Terry was a leading Bledsoe County citizen who had seen Murrell in prison in Nashville.

"Meeting between Murrell and Stewart"
from *National Police Gazette*, Dec. 19, 1846

"Scott Terry talks him into coming to Pikeville," Knight says. "At the time, before the Civil War, Pikeville was a pretty up-and-coming little town—very nice looking, with buildings and prosperous people, a very wealthy little farming community. Maybe he knew somebody here. Some people think he had distant relatives here. He came into town on the day there were some candidates here making a big speech, and [the crowd] left to see John A. Murrell. The people of the town would follow him around."

He struck up a friendship with leading citizen John Billingsley and other respectable Bledsoe County residents. "It's interesting to me," says Knight, "that here are the most prominent and well-educated people in Pikeville, and they find him interesting to talk to and befriend him. He naturally made a big impression on everybody."

Murrell regularly attended a church north of town, where the congregation praised him for his melodious bass voice. Some say it was the Baptist church, while others say Methodist or Church of Christ. He even taught Sunday school, drawing on his vast knowledge of scripture. This time, everyone felt sure, he *really* believed. He settled down to a virtuous life.

His new life was a short one. Unable to defeat the white plague, tuberculosis, he drew close to death's door. Lying in his bed above the Poston Drugstore in downtown Pikeville, he was tended by compassionate townsmen. He told his benefactor, John Billingsley, that doctors from Nashville wanted his head for medical study. Murrell, once so proud, may have felt flattered, though dread would probably have been a more likely reaction.

Murrell again confessed to the crimes of horse and slave stealing but still insisted he had never murdered anyone. "He said he never killed anybody that didn't need killing. Or that he never killed anybody that didn't try to kill him first," says Knight.

He died Sunday, November 3, 1844. The men in Pikeville took their Christian duty seriously in preparing the repentant outlaw's broken body for burial. They shaved, bathed, and dressed him with care, says Knight. "They said he was not branded, nor was there any scar [on his thumb]. But he had definite noticeable scars on his fingers." These scars were noted as identifying marks in his prison record. "A. P. Green, a carpenter by trade, made Murrell a plain coffin out of black walnut and covered it with black velvet. As soon as he completed the coffin, he removed his coat, boots, and hat and lay down in the coffin. After lying there a few seconds, he arose and said that he had done what no other man on earth had or ever would do—he had lain in the coffin of John A. Murrell."

John Billingsley, ill himself, had Murrell's body pulled several miles by sled to the family burial ground, now known as Smyrna Cemetery. "They buried him in an unmarked grave turned north-and-south instead of the usual east-and-west position, to designate he was not a law-abiding citizen," says Knight. Christians were traditionally buried facing east so they could see Christ on Resurrection Day. Although Murrell had repented and was taken into the church as a true believer, accounts of the burial consistently claim he was denied an east-facing interment. Perhaps he himself requested the unholy angle, says a neighbor, as penitence for his many sins. According to legend, a large, unadorned stone slab was placed over the grave to keep Murrell down.

Notice of his death made the Nashville paper by November 21. "That's when somebody thought they could get some money for his head," says Robnett. "So he comes to Jasper, Tennessee, and employs a young doctor down there. They come to Pikeville in a buggy or carryall, they call it. They don't go to the Billingsleys. The Billingsleys buried him—they wouldn't have approved of it. They went into the grave that night and took his head, just his head. I talked to the descendant of the doctor who came from Jasper. He was a young doctor, and he handed that down. These two men are going into strange territory. They've got to have local help. They go to the Worthington Plantation, which is near there, and enlisted a slave."

Robnett's mother said her friend "Aunt Eva"—John Billingsley's youngest daughter—told her that, later, every time the act was mentioned, an old slave from the Worthington Plantation would laugh. "They suspicioned that

"They took the body, one by the heels and one by the head, and heaved it out over the edge of the Ravine."
A print from *The Life and Adventures of John A. Murrell* by H.R. Howard, 1845

somebody had to direct these men at night in a territory where they'd never been. They suspicioned that he was the one."

Crossing Rankin Branch damaged the carryall, forcing them to show themselves in the community. "They had to have an axle or something repaired," says Robnett. "Two men, strange men, came to this blacksmith over at Cold Springs, the little village on [US] 127. And the blacksmith did the repair." The smith sent them on their way but commented afterward that the vehicle emitted a foul odor and was swarming with green flies—the kind attracted to dead flesh.

After traveling several miles south, the head snatchers spent the night in the hotel in Pikeville. "Somebody was suspicious, and they alerted Mr. Billingsley," says Knight. "He did everything he could to get the head back."

But the graverobbers did reach Jasper with the head, says Robnett. "Some people said they charged ten cents apiece to peep in the carryall and look at the head. The head is supposed to have gone to Nashville to Vanderbilt, but Vanderbilt was not there at the time." Robnett has also read that the head went to Philadelphia.

Accounts circulated about a medical examination of the skull. Some described it as a fine, perfectly shaped specimen. Medical students found nothing abnormal except its size. It was unusually large and heavy, weighing an ounce or two more than Daniel Webster's. This meant, according to the science of the time, that Murrell was far beyond the average human in mental powers.

A museum in Nashville supposedly has his mummified finger. "They might have taken his finger," Knight says. "If you would take somebody's head, it wouldn't be much trouble to take his fingers."

Murrell had fallen from celebrity to sideshow freak. It's possible the head never made it into the academic realm, where it would have been accorded some respectability through its value to science. Instead, wrote Margaret Hollinshead to author Paul Wellman, "the severed head became so noisome it was buried again, I do not know where."

"They *never* found it," Robnett says.

Most likely, somewhere off a back road in Middle Tennessee, beneath the hooves of cattle or the roots of a wizened tree, John Murrell's head has returned to dust. Miles away, his mutilated body has rotted in the ground of Smyrna Cemetery. Even the slab marking the grave was violated. Curiosity seekers chipped at the stone, taking pieces away as macabre souvenirs.

Some folks around Bledsoe County began to murmur that Murrell's soul was uneasy. Tales were told that, after dark, a headless apparition walked aimlessly among the cairns and headstones of the graveyard, seeking its head and lost treasure. Regardless of Murrell's quest—head or gold—eternal rest eluded him.

Once again, the citizens of Bledsoe County took pity on Murrell. In the 1950s or 1960s, people were coming through the fields asking where his grave was, says Robnett. "Jim Brown took up a dollar here and there down at Standefer's Drugstore." He collected enough to place a simple stone on the grave imprinted only with the outlaw's name.

Today, John Murrell's burial spot atop a gentle knoll remains alone, apart from the other graves, under the small marker among the tall cedar trees. The original flat rock lies there still, under the grass, holding him down. Or does it?

MURRELL'S TREASURE IN SALE CREEK

After Murrell's death, men throughout the South pondered one question: Where is the treasure? Everyone thought the "Reverend Devil" had booty, mostly gold, hidden in one or more holes or caves. And many a shovel was broken looking for it.

It was told around Sale Creek that Murrell buried gold there. Historian Curtis Coulter learned from resident Mark David Alexander about rumors that Murrell had been spotted in the area. Being well known, Murrell tried to steer clear of the law by avoiding railroad tracks and other widely used routes. He traveled to the foot of Bakewell Mountain and over into Sale Creek. Having murdered his partners, he rode alone with two horses, one for him and one for the gold. When the packhorse grew lame under the weight of treasure, Murrell had to unload it and bury the gold on the spot, under a three-pronged poplar tree. Then he left the valley.

In truth, there is no evidence Murrell ever came to Sale Creek. No railroad existed in Sale Creek before Murrell's death in 1844. But for years after his quiet demise, few knew what had happened to him. Rumors even circulated he was killed years later in Arkansas.

Not knowing he had died years before, could the Sale Creek witnesses have seen the ghost of John A. Murrell? If so, he had been reunited with his head and his treasure.

A shadowy figure lingered beneath the
dead oak on the Briceland Homestead.

shadow man

VAN BUREN COUNTY, TENNESSEE

*A tree that appears aged and decaying might seem beauti-
ful and inviting to the spirit who remembers a time when
both were young and pulsing with life. The dark entity
hovering near the soil into which this ancient oak once
pushed its roots may believe he's still resting in the gentle
breeze beneath its boughs.*

A large tree spreading wide over a forest of leggy saplings
speaks of the time when it stood alone above an open field,
unhindered by its fellows. Almost always, a tree like this grew
near a house, a barn, or a fence line and, by design or neglect,
was spared the ax when all around its kindred fell.

Such a tree once stretched across the wooded patch of
land off TN 30 up the mountain from Pikeville, near Fall
Creek Falls. Jack and Carol Briceland chose to homestead
here in the mid-1990s. It was an oak tree, they think, and long
dead. The twigs had rotted away, leaving only the rough bole

and several large, blunted limbs. Its age was unknown, but oak trees in the Tennessee mountains often live more than two hundred years.

The Bricelands settled on a site for their new home—the same site on which a fated acorn had fallen centuries before. Reluctantly, they agreed that what remained of the tree would have to go—eventually. In the meantime, the house plan took shape on paper, and the old tree waited.

Carol, just moved from Ohio and curious about the neighborhood, started looking into the history of the area. "That's when this ghost started appearing," she says. "I could feel the presence but actually didn't see the image or the shadow." She sensed a connection between him and the oak tree, wondering if he had been hanged from its once-sturdy limbs. "To me, it looked like a hanging tree," says Carol.

She and Jack weren't eager to cut the old sentinel down, but the time came to break ground. Soon, heavy equipment scraped the tree's stout stump aside, along with the soil that had nurtured it for untold years, and began the basement excavation.

But the entity remained. Having sensed a vague presence for some time, Carol finally caught sight of it out of the corner of her eye. "I saw this shadow and I thought, *Oh, come on, Carol! Nah, can't be.* At different times, I would feel this presence and then catch a glimpse of him. His coat was tattered around the bottom and hung below his hips like a work coat or maybe a Civil War jacket. It could've just been a shirttail hanging out. His clothes were just hanging on him, like they wore back in those days."

She thought he might have been a soldier or a Civil War veteran and named him Johnny. Carol estimates that Johnny stood at least six feet tall. "I'm five-six, and he was quite a bit taller than I was. And he was thin. I couldn't make out his face and couldn't tell about his hair at all. From a side view, he seemed to have a flat nose."

Carol kept the news of the shadow man's visitations from her husband. But Jack found out soon enough. While cutting boards in the basement one afternoon, wrapped in a cloud of sawdust, he noticed a man standing near his side. He removed his dust mask and asked, "You looking for work? Or something to eat?" He quickly realized that no one stood there—the figure's evaporation before his eyes provided evidence of that. Jack convinced himself that sawdust had swirled into a shape and blown out the door.

Carol knows when the shadow man is near. "The hair on the back of your neck stands up. It's kind of a cold feeling. I've felt him more than I've seen him. We've been here ten years, and he's been here probably six of the last ten years."

He's come in the house, she says, usually at Christmastime or New Year's. "One year, after Christmas, I was out in the kitchen baking a cake, and I felt his presence. I jokingly said, 'Well, Johnny, I hope you like carrot cake because that's what we're having for dessert tonight.' Then the feeling was gone. There was a piece missing in the morning, but I'm sure my son ate it."

Johnny doesn't worry the Bricelands at all. "I've never been afraid of ghosts," says Carol. "I'd like to make friends with him."

The shadow man wanted to cozy up with her, too. One day, Carol heard someone walking on the front porch, so she went to the door. Her big cat, Dog, went along. "All of a sudden, [Dog] screamed and tore back down the cellar steps," she says. "It was such an eerie sound. I had never heard her do it before and never heard her do it again. That's when I felt the hand on my head. It was very definite. It startled me." The hand ran down the back of her head to the nape of her neck. Carol wasn't afraid, though she was angry. "I just blurted out, 'Don't you ever touch me again!' I didn't mean to snap out at him like that. Maybe I *was* afraid. It didn't seem like I was afterwards, though." She is not worried when the sound of footsteps still comes now and then from the front and back porches.

The Bricelands, like many rural people, sleep with their windows open to enjoy the clean smell of the earth and the cool night air. Late one evening, the smell of cigar smoke awakened Carol. "I'm always leery of somebody throwing a cigarette out and the woods catching fire," she says. But she knows it was a cigar because she well remembers the time she smoked one and made herself sick. "I used to smoke cigarettes, so it wasn't that smell." Nobody smokes at her house. Does she have a neighbor fond of cigars? If so, the wind must have been powerful—the Bricelands built right in the middle of fifty acres. From any window, they view trees, trees, and more trees. People traveling the roads weren't the culprits either. The Bricelands live a good six hundred feet off TN 30, which sees little traffic these days, and about two hundred feet off Austin Lane, which bears almost no traffic at all.

So who or what haunts the Briceland house? According to some observers of the paranormal, entities known as "shadow people" are becoming more widely reported. They're seen most often around houses, although they are sometimes spotted outside. One type appears in human form. They can be very tall and sometimes wear hats. People often see them out of the corners of their eyes or as reflections in shiny surfaces and mirrors. As Carol found out, cats are sensitive to them. Although shadow people are suspected by some to be demons because of their dark forms and occasional red eyes, most investigators believe they are ghosts.

Carol has tried to solve the mystery of the shadow man. If he is but a dim remnant of flesh and blood, who was he? The area boasts a colorful history. "It was part of the old Sparta Road," says Bledsoe County librarian Carolyne Knight. "Early on, practically everyone had to come through here."

"We heard they would sneak slaves through on the old road, hiding them in a false floor in the wagons," says Jack

Briceland. "And there's a rumor some guy buried gold up here."

The most famous person to live in the area, albeit briefly, was the outlaw John A. Murrell. He was hired on at the Mitchell place as a blacksmith after his release from the Nashville Penitentiary in 1844. "We're at the old Ed Davis farm," Carol says. "The farm behind us, maybe half a mile to the south, is the Mitchell place. I know because neighbors referred to the barn that's sitting back there as 'the Mitchell barn.' "

Could the dark ghost be the outlaw? Chances are good that Murrell once walked the hardwood forest of what is now the Briceland homestead. Folks treated him well on the mountain, they say, and he was likely grateful to the Mitchells for taking him in. Carol named the shadow man Johnny before ever hearing of John Murrell. Buried gold is often associated with Murrell. And such a man, having been trapped within prison walls for ten years, might well long to linger under the broad, shady arms of a summer-dressed oak.

Spell of the Shadow

When I visit haunted places, I am looking for ghost stories, not ghosts. At the Bricelands', I found more than I came for. My tape recorder, having operated flawlessly for months, abruptly refused to work there, even after a battery change. I could barely work myself, almost falling asleep while sitting at the dining-room table, only feet from where the old tree once grew. But as I reached for my coat and said my good-byes, my husband, Dan, impatiently pushed the record button one more time. The tape began to roll.

What had happened? Did the shadow man interfere with my recorder and try to lull me to sleep? I had heard of equipment malfunctions during paranormal investigations but had never experienced one. I can only surmise that the shadow man is bashful. I beg his indulgence in telling his tale.

the pitty pat

SALE CREEK, TENNESSEE

Entities that pursue and hitchhike are well-known arche-
types in ghost lore. But sometimes, what is assumed a
quaint myth may well spring forth with new life, terrifying
a person who has never heard such stories. Can a belief in
something by many people over many years finally make it
real? Or do some archetypes, contrary to what the profes-
sors believe, derive from reality rather than a communal
imagination?

Like all white men entering new lands, pioneers settling
northern Hamilton County followed trails made by Native
Americans, who followed trails carved by deer and buffalo
before them. One such trail became known as Shipley Hollow
Road. It snakes through the hills, starting at Daugherty Ferry
Road off US 27, then dead-ends at Providence Road after a
climb up through the dark woods.

The settlers chose a spot among the trees on a knoll
midway along the route for their cemetery. Many who had trod

the road below laid down their bones within the cemetery's leafy borders. Some slumber beneath no more than mossy quilts, with no stones to bear witness to the lives that once were.

In those days, the old road was just two ruts in the wilderness, winding through a living tunnel of oak and laurel limbs that dimmed the sunlight. At night, walkers and riders had no streetlights to show the way through the blackness that swallowed up the countryside. Houses were few and far between. But all country roads were such then, and people went about their business.

Until somebody or something awoke in the 1860s.

A woman and her two children were making their way north in a wagon toward the hollow one foggy night. The woman had likely made the trip many times, as it would have been unusual for a mother and children to travel alone in the dark in strange territory. No one remembers her name or the purpose of her errand that night. But most old people in the area know the story of her death, says historian Curtis Coulter, author of *Down Country Roads: Stories of Sale Creek, Tennessee.*

As she and her children drew near the fork in the road, tells Curtis, something pounced on them out of the black. The horse bolted, wrecking the wagon and crushing the woman to death. The shadowy creature snatched the children, who were never seen again.

Soon thereafter, folks began hearing *pitty pat, pitty pat, pitty pat* along the dirt road. Was it the creature? "They'd turn around, and there'd be nothing there," says Curtis. "Sometimes, they would run from it. For this reason, most of the people who lived in the hollow were good sprinters."

The elusive Pitty Pat hunts anytime from dusk to pitch dark. "It was told as the truth that people got their business done early so they didn't have to be out on the road at night," Curtis says. "They would go all the way around the hollow to keep from having to go through it."

Curtis's own great-grandfather had an encounter with the entity. One evening in the 1880s as Dr. Downey rode up through the hollow to call on a patient, something leaped on the horse with him. Though he couldn't see it, he thought it catlike. "He felt like he was being attacked," says Curtis. "Of course, the horse went to bucking. He was able to get it off and stay on the horse. He went on up the hollow and got to his patient's house. He told them if they had a room he was just going to stay there because he wasn't going back through the hollow." Another doctor, Jack Kennedy, had the same experience not long after that and also invited himself to stay the night with a patient.

But doctors weren't the only people on the road after dark. "One of the Elseas lived up in there right across the ridge in Elsea Hollow," tells Curtis. "He was going up past the Mill Dam area, and it got after him. He stopped at a man's house who lived along in there and asked to spend the night. When told there was only one bed, Elsea told him just to move over, that he was sleeping with him because he wasn't going up to that hollow by himself that night."

An elderly lady, Mrs. Reynolds, was heading up the hill near the hollow when something got on the back of her buggy. "It was like it was lugging [slowing] the buggy down, and the little horse almost couldn't pull the hill. When they got to the top of the hill, it was gone. It hopped off," Curtis says.

"I don't know if anybody ever pinned it down because they was running too hard to get away," Curtis says, smiling. Through the years, Pitty Pat frights would fade for a while before returning to hapless travelers in the Shipley Hollow area.

In the 1950s, two men—members of the Francisco and Iles families, says Curtis—experienced a similar terror in exactly the same place a few years apart.

"They'd been working at night and were coming home. When you turn off at Daugherty Ferry Road, go out there about three-fourths of a mile. Right before you come to the little bridge, there's a bank on the right. Both of them said they were coming along there and something dark darted off of the bank. One of them said it hit the side of his car on the passenger side. He just took off, it scared him so bad. He went up to one of the neighbors' houses and got them. They got a flashlight out and checked his car."

Despite what had felt like a powerful collision, the man couldn't find a scratch, a dent, blood, hair, or any other evidence that something had collided with the car. So the men took the flashlight and examined the scene. "They hunted all along the road because he said, as hard as that hit, it would've killed anything." Again, nothing turned up suggesting an animal had even crossed through the brush, much less met a violent death in the road.

A decade later, another of Curtis's relatives met up with the Pitty Pat. "When I was a senior in high school, in the winter of '67," he says, "we had a ball game one night. One of my cousins and her girlfriend always ran around together, so my cousin was going to take her home. They had to cross this bridge—this would have been two to three hundred yards from where Francisco and Iles had their experiences. When they

The girls saw a strange green light in the water beneath the Mill Dam Bridge on Daugherty Ferry Road.

got to the bridge and were crossing, one of them just happened to look over to the right and down in the water. They said it was like two big glowing green eyes looking up at 'em. Dell said she threw the '53 Chevy up in second gear and took off. She took Phyllis home, put her out, and she can't remember how she got home.

"A bunch of boys had been swimming just past the bridge and headed up Daugherty Ferry Road and had not gotten to Shipley Hollow yet. They heard something over in the woods, and they had a footrace to the first house, and all of 'em just ran in the house and slammed the door." It is unknown how the occupants took to this unusual home invasion. By then, folks had likely grown accustomed to people house-crashing while fleeing the Pitty Pat.

Curtis thinks all the Pitty Pat talk is just folklore, created in a time when people didn't have television and had to entertain themselves by spinning tall tales. "I don't put a lot of credence in it. I count it as legend because I don't believe in ghosts," says Curtis. "I think most of it was people's imagination going wild. I suspect that it was either a bobcat or a panther." He remembers the time a bobcat jumped on a man on a tractor. The man's wife killed it. Curtis saw the dead cat with his own eyes. "There are sightings of large cats around here even now."

However, he is hard-put to explain an encounter by hunters in November 2004. "I had a man stop here the Wednesday before Thanksgiving. He was an investigator from the Dunedin Fire Department in Florida."

The man told Curtis he had been hunting nearby.

"Yeah, I saw you in there," Curtis said.

The man said, "I understand you've written a book with the Pitty Pat creature in it." He then told a story that made even the skeptical Curtis a bit uneasy.

"He and his partner went in there and got in the tree stand," recalls Curtis, "and it was still pitch dark. They had walkie-talkies and talked back and forth."

The man's friend called him and said, "The deer have already started to move." That was strange because it was too dark and early for deer to begin their day. But the friend insisted. "I can *hear* them moving through the woods."

"Then he got static and he couldn't hear [his friend] anymore," says Curtis. "In about five minutes, he heard something come down the woods. He looked, and it was something that looked blacker than the woods themselves. It turned toward him and kept coming toward his tree. The next thing he knew, it was just like it was breathing down his neck. He was too scared to do anything. In about five minutes, it was gone.

"After this happened, he began checking around to see if there were any kind of tales. He said, 'I'm not a nut.' He went to a bookstore up there, and they had a copy of my book. Then he came and asked me about it."

The encounter happened two ridges west of Shipley Hollow. "But that's basically the same thing we've heard about the Pitty Pat," Curtis says. "It's consistent with some of the

The Shipley Hollow Cemetery is no place to be after sunset.

Pitty Pat tales. That one has as much credence as any I've heard."

The Pitty Pat may have expanded its territory. According to Curtis, you might meet the creature anywhere along Daugherty Ferry Road starting just south of the Mill Dam Bridge, going across the bridge and around the curve, continuing to where Daugherty Ferry forks off into Shipley Hollow Road, and extending up Shipley Hollow, particularly around the Shipley Cemetery, on the right.

People driving cars can hope for some protection from the entity. But those on foot, bicycle, or horseback would be well advised to limit their meanderings up the hollow to daytime. The Pitty Pat still lurks in the deep shadows just beyond the quiet country roads of Sale Creek.

Little Nina Craigmiles
Photo courtesy of St. Luke's Episcopal
Church, Cleveland, Tennessee

the tears of little nina

CLEVELAND, TENNESSEE

*Death always saddens those left behind. But sadder still is
the young soul called away with so much left undone. Small
wonder that, 135 years later, an entire town still mourns
the loss of little Nina Craigmiles.*

Little Nina Craigmiles, embracing her favorite doll,
Vivienne, flounced down the grand stairway. Her quick, tiny
footsteps fell muffled on the carpeted treads, then clicked like
a scattered string of seed pearls across the polished floor toward
the front door. Someone had just pulled up in a carriage. She
could hear the rattling harnesses and the clipped striking of
horses' hooves. She saw her mother strain against the French
beveled-glass door and nod toward the visitor. A surprise was
sure to reveal itself, she'd been promised.

The adults in Nina's life worshiped her, fussing over her

and entertaining her every whim. Well, almost. She was not allowed to go out with other little girls, and she so wanted to. She was royalty in Cleveland, a delicate beauty who would wilt in the cold world, should she be turned loose in it. John and Adelia Craigmiles hadn't even allowed Nina to host a party that August, several weeks earlier, in celebration of her seventh birthday, and they refused to give in to their daughter's pleas to attend school. How wonderful it would be, she often imagined, to lock arms with other children and go to school. She watched them skip down the street, chattering, singing, telling secrets. And laughing. She wondered what they laughed at. Sometimes, she and Vivienne giggled with them up in her ornately framed window, but the girls didn't see her.

On this keen fall Wednesday, Nina had forgotten about the children. Her grandfather was coming to take her out for a drive. Dr. Gideon B. Thompson stepped into the foyer, richly furnished in red (according to an old *Cleveland Journal* article), and reached for his granddaughter. He twirled the squealing girl, skirt floating, then set her lightly down on the outside step facing the drive.

Before her was a shiny black carriage pulled by a shiny black horse whose white blaze seemed to have been embroidered upon his face for the sole purpose of pointing to his flaring velvet nostrils.

"His name is Lighting," said Dr. Thompson.

The horse stood, his small feet tapping the gravel.

"Where's Beck?" asked Adelia, alarmed at the unexpected appearance of the black horse in place of the gentle mule. She looked toward the street as if expecting the mule to appear.

Dr. Thompson didn't answer. He took Nina's hand and strutted around the carriage, delighting in her approval of it.

"Can I ride in it? Please?" Nina said.

"Not only may you ride in it, little one, but you may also invite Vivienne along." He bowed to Nina and her doll, whose bisque head was coiffed with a wig of real hair the same sable brown as Nina's own. Nina cradled the doll in her arms, its silk skirts falling over hers.

"Oh, no," said Adelia, running after her daughter. "No, darling. Not today."

Adelia ran her fingers over Nina's dark curls, then held the child's soft face between milky hands, frowning. Looking up at her mother, Nina let her lower lip droop. A deep breath escaped Adelia, signaling her defeat.

"Nina, you are not to drive today. Do you understand me? And you," she continued, looking at Dr. Thompson, "are not to let her drive. I must insist on this." She gave her father her sternest look. "Promise me."

"I promise," he said with mock seriousness.

Nina looked up at the high carriage seat. "Now can we ride in it?"

"That horse looks quite unreliable," Adelia said, snatching Nina's hand.

"Don't you think I can handle my own horse?" her father said. "Let the little one have her fun. And I've already promised *her* we'll go riding today."

Adelia knew she had to let Nina go. If she couldn't trust her own father with her daughter, whom could she trust? And besides, Nina went out with him on rounds all the time.

Her grandfather swung Nina up into the leather seat. She held up the doll's arm to wave at her mother, still standing in the drive.

"We'll be back directly," Dr. Thompson said as he snapped the reins.

Off they trotted toward downtown Cleveland. "Faster!" Nina yelled.

Dr. Thompson allowed the horse to pick up the pace.

"Let me drive," she said.

"No, little one, I gave my word. You heard me," he said unevenly as they bounced along.

"Please!" Nina squealed.

"We'll drive together," he said, "just for a minute."

Nina wrapped her little hands tightly around the reins, taking care to cradle Vivienne tightly with her elbow. Faster and faster they went. Nina and Dr. Thompson laughed. They careened around one corner, then another.

"Faster!" Nina yelled.

They approached the railroad tracks—wheels clattering, harness jingling, hoofbeats grinding—bearing down on the crossing at Central Avenue ahead. Still laughing, they didn't hear danger—steel on steel roaring toward them—until too late.

Dr. Thompson jerked the reins and grabbed for the brake. "Whoa!"

The carriage skidded one way, then the other, pulling the horse off balance but slowing him, too. Then, as the train blasted its warning whistle, the horse bolted forward in panic. The switch engine slammed into the carriage just as it jolted over the tracks. It killed Nina, crushing her under the cowcatcher, and smashed her Vivienne to ivory shards. Dr. Thompson was thrown clear and cursed with the unhappy fate of those who find themselves alive when others die.

A shock wave rolled over the town, described by the Reverend George James in St. Alban's Episcopal Church's historical register: "A thrill of horror runs through the whole community, the whole town mourns the sad fate of the universal favorite, and sympathizes with the afflicted and doating [sic] parents, who are driven to distraction by the loss of their only child. Nina was an affectionate, sweet and charitable child."

Two days later, the Reverend James eulogized Nina: "Today, our little chapel is draped in mourning; business is suspended, and nearly all the town attends the funeral of sweet little Nina. The coffin is placed close to the chancel rail. The font is enclosed in flowers and drapes. The room filled up with saddened friends, the windows are surrounded with eager faces."

Only someone who has suffered the death of a cherished child can know how devastated the Craigmiles and Thompson families were, how they mourned the sounds of lyrical chatter and the reciting of simple verse, the sweet scents of soap and clean hair, the feel of small fingers curled in theirs, the look of soft lashes over dark eyes—all those tiny things that add up to a child.

They say the family never got over it, not really. Less than two years later, Dr. Thompson died, no doubt hurried to the grave by guilt and grief. John and Adelia Craigmiles vowed never to forget their daughter and offered God a gift in her memory. Three years after Nina's death, on October 18, 1874, St. Luke's Episcopal Church opened its doors at 320 Broad Street thanks to a donation from her parents. A Carrara marble mausoleum almost as costly as the church itself stands in the churchyard. Its four-foot-thick walls shelter the remains of Nina Craigmiles, tucked into a sculpted marble sarcophagus in the heart of the monument, surrounded by the peaceful, soft light of Jesus cradling a lamb within the stained glass circling the ceiling.

Cleveland's children still believe Little Nina haunts the mausoleum where she and her family are laid to rest.

Over the years, Nina was joined by her infant brother, who died hours after birth, nameless, then by her father, who died of blood poisoning after a fall on South Street, and then by her mother, killed by a car in front of her Church Street home. All were interred around Nina.

Some remember that she was preserved in a glass-covered coffin because her parents could not bear to hide her away. Anyone who entered could see her. But eventually, perhaps after her parents' deaths or due to the deterioration of her little body, the story went, Nina's face was covered.

It is rumored that, later, the family ordered a fine marble statue of Nina from an Italian sculptor to fill a niche in the church sanctuary. But the sculpture was lost at sea, sinking into the icy, black waters of the Atlantic in 1912, entombed within the *Titanic*. If so, the family must have felt the sting of her loss all over again.

This tale does not lack merit. Although there is no record of such a statue in the *Titanic*'s cargo manifest, it could well have been aboard a less legendary ship that sank in the Atlantic in earlier years. And it would be expected that the Craigmiles family might commission such an artwork, having the wealth to do so. Such ornaments can be found in many cemeteries and churches of that era. Why shouldn't Nina have one?

Some believe Nina still tarries in the churchyard and that, like most children, she cries sometimes. They know when she's crying, they say, because her tears stain the white marble red. Despite repeated scrubbings and even the replacement of some of the slabs, the red stains return.

Her sobs may be heard, too, coming from within the mausoleum. It's hard to know what brings forth her sorrow. Perhaps she awakens briefly to remember her short, sheltered life, or maybe she grieves over all that was meant to be but wasn't.

She has touched several generations of children. They feel a great deal of sympathy for her, says Bradley County historian emeritus Dr. William Snell. In the first few decades after Nina's interment, groups of children would often visit at lunch and walk around the carved stone wall to awaken her. Legend says if someone walks around seven times, then knocks on the door, she will answer. Or the wrought-iron gate will swing open. Or the person who knocks will die. Few children, says Dr. Snell, have ever gotten that far, always stopping just short of summoning Nina.

There are even recent stories that children have glimpsed a small girl around the churchyard dressed in late-nineteenth-century finery.

Is it Nina, still looking for playmates?

HAUNTED LIBRARY

There are those who believe the house where Nina's uncle Pleasant Craigmiles once lived is haunted, too. The majestic old Italianate home that Nina no doubt visited often during her brief life still stands at 833 Ocoee Street. While some believe Nina lingers there, others claim her grandmother went insane after the girl's death and can still be seen in her rocking chair beside the third-story tower window, looking for Nina and calling her to come home. That is not likely, says Barbara Fagen, manager of the History Branch of the Cleveland Public Library. The grand windows in that room are way too high for anyone to look out.

All of the Craigmiles clan, once the most influential family in Cleveland, are long dead, says Dr. Snell. Their historic house now serves as the History Branch of the library.

lost in toyland

HIXSON, TENNESSEE

A motherless child plucks at the heartstrings, but sadder yet is the child separated from her parents even in death. Such orphaned spirits forget their loneliness for a brief time, indulging in play and mischief. But always, tears return to forlorn little eyes.

In the early spring of 1989, a new department store prepared to open in the Northgate area. Workmen labored every day to tear out the old interior of the building so they could renovate it to suit the new tenant. But the men weren't whistling while they worked. There was a feeling of unease among the crew, a sense that something eerie was present—intangible, but barely. The third-shift crew was especially edgy. Still, they kept up their pace, eager to finish the project.

Then real problems developed. When the crew reported to work, they often found their neatly stored tools in disarray. Apparently, vandals had entered the structure when no one was on duty and strewn hammers, drills, and extension cords around the workspace. Oddly, nothing was missing. It happened again, then again. The men were getting angry, but they were unable to gather any clues about the perpetrators' identities or how they had entered the building. All the doors were kept locked, even when the men were there. There were only two ways out—the main door, which required a manager's key to open, and the emergency exits, wired to alert the fire department if opened.

One evening, all seemed well. Upon reporting for work and finding all the tools in good order, the crew entered the area in preparation to begin. Someone tossed an extension cord toward an outlet while the remaining workmen took a couple of minutes to gather other tools. Turning back toward the cord, they saw it jerk tight on its own, straight as an arrow. Their nerves stretched as taut as the cord, they warily began working, no man wanting to be out of sight or sound of the others.

Then they froze. A bell tinkled nearby. It came closer and closer, growing louder and louder. A little girl on a tricycle peddled toward them, turned the corner, and rode down the next aisle. Then she was gone as quickly as she had come.

The tough-talking construction workers abandoned all pretense and fled from the pitiful wisp of a child. They huddled together at the front of the store, waiting for the night manager to come at five in the morning and let them out. When the door finally opened, the startled manager was nearly stampeded by his men. They ran past him out the door and never returned.

Finally, the work was completed and the store opened. Customers enjoyed the bright and cheery décor. But among the buzz of people shopping and employees working, two lost children wandered the aisles. Or did they? When employees walked toward the distant children—an unkempt small boy and a slightly older girl in a scruffy little dress—they seemed to evaporate, leaving the witnesses to question their eyes and their sanity.

A sense that children were about permeated the store. One morning, a manager came in early to open up. Assuming that another staff member would arrive about thirty minutes later, as usual, he was surprised to see evidence that the man had already come in—his children were scampering about at the end of an aisle. Later, he commented to the man that he'd seen his children. The employee was miffed. "I don't have any children," he said. Furthermore, he was not even there at the time the children were seen. No one was on the premises but the manager.

Despite a struggle to keep the toy department neat, inventory would not stay on the shelves. The rest of the store remained just as employees left it when they went home each evening, but the toy department was frequently in disarray the next morning. The department manager was at wit's end. Senior management feared that a family was squatting in the store. An investigation uncovered no evidence to support that theory. Toys were often out of place in the stockroom also. When employees entered the area in the morning, they might discover a doll, out of its box or wrapper, sitting in the middle of the floor. One worker looked up to see a little girl dart around a corner and disappear.

A former employee says the mysterious waifs did not spend all their time playing. One day while working in her office, Sheila Thompson heard a child crying in the bathroom. Sheila is known as being very sensitive to the needs of children. She tends her own children and everybody else's. So she went to check. No one was in the ladies' room. She called the security guard to check the men's room. Still no child. Outside in the shopping area, she could not hear the crying. She chalked it up to sound carrying through the ventilation system and tried to forget about it.

But the distraught child would not be silent. Over the course of several years, Sheila heard the same voice crying. "It wasn't a I'm-not-getting-my-way kind of cry," she says. "It was a wailing, troubled-child cry, a suffering child." She pauses. "I'm getting the chills just talking about this." She has to collect herself before continuing. "At least fifteen times, I tried to get a coworker to hear this. But as soon as he showed up, the crying stopped. Every time."

One other person did hear it, though. During a training session, a new employee came racing around the corner toward the bathroom—"real wide-eyed," Sheila says.

"Some child is hurt somewhere!" the trainee screamed. In a panic, the woman flew into the men's restroom without even checking to see if it was occupied. After looking in the ladies' room, she hurried to Sheila's office. "They've *got* to be in the stockroom," she said.

Sheila knew they would find no child. But the employee insisted they continue the search, so Sheila set out once again. As always, the search was fruitless. Although Sheila had long ago given up looking for the disembodied sobs, she still avoided entering the stockroom alone. "I was always unnerved," she says.

No one knows who the two lost children might be. The haunted building sits on what was a cornfield before the shopping center was built in the 1980s. Hixson was a quiet community once, its small businesses and farms dotting the gently rolling hills north of the Tennessee River. The field was part of a farm belonging to John H. Hixson before it was sold to the Tallent family in the late 1930s or early 1940s, says John H. Hixson's great-grandson Don Vandergriff. Close by was a frame farmhouse, most likely accompanied by a barn, corncribs, a smokehouse, a chicken house, and a hogpen, all long gone.

It was not uncommon for such a farmstead to have a cemetery nearby. If the farmer was of modest means, the grieved-over graves may have been unmarked or marked only with rocks. If the family was fortunate enough to be able to afford engraved headstones, the inscriptions may have quickly worn if they were carved in soft limestone or sandstone. Finally, brambles would have overcome the little family plot and hidden it from view, leaving it vulnerable to bush hogs and bulldozer blades.

All over the Tennessee Valley, graves have been lost forever in just this way. Many of these graves contained the earthly remains of children, who died frequently in the decades before vaccines and antibiotics. Back then, diseases that are unknown or merely inconvenient today—whooping cough, influenza, yellow fever, and even simple infections—snatched many a child from the desperate arms of an anguished mother.

What of the children plucked from those warm arms? Two of them lost their way and lingered awhile, wandering the aisles of a department store in search of home, family, and a final resting place, all gone forever.

a ghost gets revenge

SIGNAL MOUNTAIN, TENNESSEE

Those of flesh and blood haunted by supernatural beings frequently conspire to cast them out, in hopes of freeing themselves of interference from the other side. But a spirit who has been betrayed and ill-used by the living might turn the tables on an unwary perpetrator. Exorcism can go both ways.

Oscar Carlson believed someone was trying to kill him. Not that he had any enemies. A well-liked man on Walden's Ridge in 1919, he was often seen bouncing around the Summertown roads in his Model T Ford, smoking a pipe held with the stub of a missing index finger. No one imagined that this reclusive, industrious farmer would come to a violent end at his own home.

It was late July. Carlson's forty-acre farm on south Sawyer Road must have looked like a verdant cornucopia to admiring neighbors—or envious ones. Carlson cultivated two acres in fruit trees. Nearby stood one of the finest barns on the mountain. A windmill whose *click-clack* could be heard around the neighborhood pumped water to all parts of the property through an elaborate system the Swedish immigrant had engineered himself. Carlson's well-built two-story house was one of several handsome homes he had constructed in the Summertown area. It boasted a rock front and steps, a root cellar, and a detached garage—a rarity at the time. In that garage was the one-seat Model T.

Carlson, too, was in the garage that fateful night. He had taken to sleeping there, he told acquaintances, because attempts were being made on his life. Unknown persons had tried to pump gas into his house, he claimed. And someone had poisoned his well. He had no family or boarders living with him, so he locked his house and bedded down for the night next to his Ford. Then his suspicions became a horrifying reality.

The murderers went straight for the garage. The locks on the house were not tampered with—they knew exactly where to find Carlson. How they knew remains a mystery. Perhaps they spied on his activities while hatching their plot. Wooded ravines bordered the property on two sides, offering numerous opportunities for concealment. Or perhaps he trusted them, confiding the whereabouts of his hiding place.

Carlson must have known they were there, for he began dressing. Maybe he even warily opened the door. But before he was fully clad, the men fell on him and wrested his own automatic shotgun out of his hands. Three shots were fired in the struggle, none of which found a sure mark. The outnumbered Carlson went down fighting for his life before the crack of a board over his head stilled him. His skull was split in a neat line from just over his nose to the back of his neck.

The killers wrapped Carlson's half-dressed body, including one shoe, in two quilts, loaded it into his own car, then disposed of it by throwing it from East Brow Road over the bluff near the W Road, about three miles away. It would have stayed there indefinitely had the killers not botched the job. Instead of dropping five hundred feet into a tangled, impenetrable wilderness, the corpse caught on a shelf. Several children discovered it three days later. After lying in the sweltering July heat, the body had begun to decompose. Carlson's earthly remains could be identified only by the absence of two fingers and a shoe matching the one back in the garage, reported the *Daily Times*. The remains were sent to Chattanooga for autopsy.

Meanwhile, a man named Simons took possession of the property but had to instruct his large family to move into the deserted home without him, as he was soon thereafter "languishing in jail with no person willing to go his bond," according to the *Chattanooga Times*. The charge involved "certain documents by authority of which he essayed to take possession of the place."

Simons was unpopular in the community. One elderly neighbor remembered him as "the kind of person who slunk around, a spooky kind of person, who was not bright but mean." Oddly enough, Simons presented evidence that Carlson had deeded the entire homestead to him. The documented reasons for his inheritance from Carlson were "love and affection." Folks were suspicious about this. However, the authorities finally concluded that the deed had been properly executed and registered at the courthouse the year before.

At first, finding that Carlson's pockets had been turned wrong side out, the police did not believe the murder was planned. They dismissed the murderers as bungling car thieves who killed Carlson when he awakened during a robbery. And they had no leads.

But Carlson knew. He could not rest until those who had taken his life and property were vanquished. His ghostly visitations started the first night the Simons family was in the house. They were awakened by footsteps upstairs, the floors creaking under solid thuds. They searched the house but found no one. After settling back in, they were aroused again by the measured strides of the formless prowler pacing the floorboards above them. The intruder apparently walked to the window and exited into the night, heedless of the fact that the ground lay well below him. The next morning, the harassment continued, the family constantly closing and locking windows, then finding them open soon thereafter.

The worst was yet to come. One evening, Carlson materialized, appearing as he had in life. "The onlookers were shocked, terrified and petrified," stated the *Chattanooga Times*. The figure entered the garage, unmindful of the tightly latched door. The sounds of a struggle followed, after which the doors burst open. Next came the sound of three muted shots. Then two men walked out carrying what seemed to be a man's body, which they laid aside while the Ford was backed out of the garage. They loaded their burden into the car. With lights out, they drove to Sawyer Road, turned right, and, flipping the headlights on, hurried toward the bluff. The chilling pantomime was not over. The horrified Simons family watched as a transparent white form rose about four feet from the ground, remained a few moments, then disappeared once the car passed out of sight and sound.

That night, the shaken family remained in the house. The next evening, the gruesome vision was repeated. When the scenario began again the third night, the family fled to a neighbor's. They returned on the fourth night, only to see the scene replayed. They quickly packed their belongings and left, never to return.

After that, four men including Simons were indicted for the murder, the primary motive being the acquisition of the Carlson farm, rather than simple robbery. They denied all charges, claiming they had only borrowed Carlson's shotgun, which was missing from the crime scene, to "shoot crows."

The critical evidence against Simons consisted of two pages of the county registrar's ledger of property transfers. Those two pages had been torn out, and their whereabouts were unknown. Sheriff Bass and officers of the criminal court diligently sought the pages, to no avail.

In 1926, seven years after the crime, the missing property transfer pages were found and returned to the registrar's office. Sherman Beck, a respected resident of North Chattanooga, revealed that a carpenter had discovered them tacked behind the weatherboarding of a house where Simons had lived during the trial. The carpenter had demolished the home three years after the trial and held onto the pages for four more years before turning them over to Beck. The state might have used the missing pages to convict Simons of murder.

Instead, Simons and two others were acquitted of all charges because most of the evidence was circumstantial and incomplete. The fourth accused, a black man, was convicted and sentenced to death because he had the victim's car and watch in his possession, even though evidence clearly suggested that more than one person had been involved in the murder. The governor, for reasons unknown, commuted the man's date with the Grim Reaper.

Still, justice had part of its day. Although the court failed to imprison the murderers of Oscar Carlson, the coveted farm reverted to his rightful heir, his sister in Sweden, and was sold. If Simons had killed Carlson as part of a plan to seize his homestead, he had failed. He could never live there.

Questions remain. Did the Simons family, out of guilt, imagine they saw a reenactment of the murder? Or did Carlson actually cross the line between life and death in a last gesture of defiance?

The man who bought the farm lost three sons to violent deaths, say old-timers. Finally, fire consumed the house. Today, nothing remains of the Carlson place but a shallow hole in a weedy horse pasture. Carlson is there no more. He need not be. He had his revenge.

the spiraling trap

SUCK CREEK, TENNESSEE

It is said that wherever men have walked the earth, so in turn have their ghosts. This tale, originating in Cherokee legend, illustrates that stories of the unquiet dead were here long before the white man brought his own accounts of restless spirits to the valleys and mountains.

Many generations before the Cherokees claimed the Tennessee Valley as their own, Ûñtsaiyi—"the Gambler"—lived on the Tennessee River at the Suck, a great whirlpool. Legend says he made his living as a gambler, challenging people to play against him rolling stone wheels with a stick. Because he was so cunning, he won almost every match. And on the rare occasion that he lost, he changed his shape and left the winner with nothing.

Anyone who passed the infamous boiling cauldron at the western skirt of Signal Mountain also gambled, staking his very life—maybe even his soul—on the whims of the swirling waters. It is told that before the white man arrived, two

49

Cherokee men paddled down the river in a canoe. When they saw the wildly circling currents ahead, they guided their craft toward the bank to wait, expecting the currents to diminish and become smooth again. But the whirlpool grew in intensity and expanded toward the men, drawing them into a watery tornado. They were tossed out of the canoe and pulled under the water, where one was seized by a great fish and disappeared forever. The other man was carried round and round, deeper and deeper, until he was caught by another current and pitched back out. He made it to shallow water and struggled to shore, exhausted.

Later, he told a horrifying tale. When he had been pulled into the innermost circle of the vortex, he could see into its depths. And there on the floor of the river, he saw a multitude of souls, who saw him, too, and beckoned to him. As their hands reached up to grasp him, the sudden change in current pulled him back from the brink, saving him from certain doom.

Not all travelers were so fortunate. In 1780, a group of pioneers came upon the violent whirlpool and, in their helplessness, were ambushed by Chief Dragging Canoe and his

Men warp a steamboat through the Suck.
Photograph of an illustration by Henry Finn, published in 1871 in volume 1 of *Picturesque America*.

band of warriors. During the fray, one man disappeared beneath the currents. The greedy water also swallowed up a day-old infant, the first recorded white baby born in Hamilton County, who was never seen again. Over the next thirteen decades, several craft, including large commercial steamers, met an unhappy fate at the Suck. People, livestock, and fortunes were lost in its watery grip.

Impatient with this persistent obstacle to commerce, mortal men conspired to defeat it. In 1905, construction began downstream of Hales Bar to calm the dangerous channel by raising the water level. Four different construction firms, one after the other, attempted to finish the dam, but a series of baffling delays and cost overrides plagued the project. Fountains tinged an eerie purple by potassium permanganate gushed up from the bedrock and penetrated the cofferdam built to seal the structure. The engineer in charge died. Some speculated that the entities within the Suck, recognizing the threat to their timeless reign, cursed the project.

Finally, the waters impounded by the completed Hales Bar Dam and later by Nickajack Dam rose and tamed the haunted whirlpool. After snatching untold numbers of travelers, the ghastly multitude beckoned no more.

All seemed well until the autumn of 1973, when, within weeks of each other, two sturdy tugs hit shoals or large rocks and sank around midnight beneath the dark currents near the whirlpool, settling on opposite shores into the deepest water within miles. The *North Star* dropped so quickly that her chief engineer was gulped up with her. The murky depths would not give up his body for three days. The *Sara E. Thomas* descended slowly, sparing her crew but settling in a bizarre pit on the river bottom. "It's lying in a pot hole—a cave-in," salvage master John Beatty told the *Chattanooga News-Free Press*. Four diving crews struggled to bring the boat up. One crew rushed a diver suffering from the bends to the emergency room. Later, Captain Beatty declared that the *Sara E. Thomas* was "the single most complicated piece of equipment we've ever brought up, as well as the deepest."

More than thirty years have since gone by without incident. Men and boats now pass over the watery haunt unknowing, seeing only their own reflections in the gentle swirls and eddies.

mary greene of the delta queen

Life is a river, or so the poets say. In the case of one feisty riverboat captain, the river was life and still is. Even after death.

Michael Matthews stands on a Chattanooga pier, admiring the riverboat *Delta Queen*. The great paddle wheel and tall stack identify her as one of a handful of vintage steamboats that still churn the big rivers, escorted by the strains of calliope music. Matthews longs to board the grande dame, to walk her ironwood decks, to climb her staircases, and to gaze over her rails at the murky pulse below. His curiosity reaches beyond a passing interest in historic boats and his background in engineering. He knows the *Delta Queen* is haunted.

Unlike so many hauntings, says Matthews, who hosted downtown ghost tours in Chattanooga in the late 1990s, it is very clear who haunts the *Delta Queen*—Captain Mary B. Greene. Found dead of natural causes aboard ship in 1949, the eighty-year-old has ignored the announcement of her permanent retirement and remains aboard. Without question, she still runs a tight ship, and nobody dares stop her. Eighty crew members tend to the safety, comfort, and entertainment of up to 174 guests under the vigilant eye of Captain Greene. Matthews says many stories have her gliding, plain as day, right past crew members. Why, it's as if she owns the place. And once she did.

As a young woman in Newport, Ohio, Mary likely had no idea that river water ran in her veins. But her high-school sweetheart and husband-to-be, Gordon Greene, kept the steamboat *H. K. Bedford*. Every time the boat stopped in Newport, tells *Delta Queen* "Riverlorian" Travis Vasconcelos, Greene paid Mary a visit. After courting about five years, Greene won her as his bride. Luckily, he got more than he bargained for.

As a new bride, Mary spent her time in the pilothouse on the "lazy bench," a spot usually reserved for pilots riding a stretch of river they were unfamiliar with, so they could observe the veterans. Sitting there to get to know her husband, Mary came to a startling realization. She told her husband, "Gordon, I think I can do this."

"He learned her the river," says Travis. "The next thing you know, she's going to get a license in 1897, one of the pioneer women of the field. She had great respect from every pilot and captain that came on those boats."

Mary Greene had been piloting boats for thirty years when the *Delta Queen* was launched in 1927. They did not meet up right away, says Travis. The steamboat regularly shuttled between California's Sacramento and San Joaquin river deltas until 1940, when the navy drafted her and painted her gray. Mary's son Tom saved the old boat from the ship breakers in 1946 and dreamed of putting her on the rivers again, this time in the East. In 1947, the *Queen* braved the rigors of ocean towing, passed through the Panama Canal—a first for a river steamboat—arrived at New Orleans, and then traveled under her own steam to Cincinnati. After a lavish makeover improved the steamer beyond even her former wedding-cake glory, Captain Mary stepped up to the helm.

The nature of the business had changed by the time Mary took over the *Delta Queen*, explains Travis. "She was very impressed with this boat. . . . But it wasn't the old Mark Twain-type packet that she was used to. The older paddle-wheelers were packet boats—workhorses of the river. We carried farm produce, livestock, freight, and passengers. In the early days, when [Mary] started, if somebody came down on the bank with something to ship and waved a white hanky at us, we'd see 'em, stop the boat, and pick up whatever they're shipping. This was a different kind of boat entirely. Instead of cargo, it carried tourists. This boat is almost 100 feet longer than packet boats and has three decks rather than two." The *Delta Queen* measures 285 by 60 feet. "We're a pretty big monster for this river."

Captain Mary came on board permanently in 1948. Her daily life on this new generation of boat was dramatically different from what she was used to, says Travis. Whereas she would have worked in the pilothouse 80 percent of the time in packet-boat days, she found herself there less and less. Her role evolved into that of hostess. "She still did a lot of steering on her own, and she still ran her own boats. But hostess—that was a position that she grew to love. She was very good at that. She had a little circle—her sewing club—that would get together every day and make all sorts of things—aprons, handkerchiefs." She would seek out the ladies on board and invite them to join in. In the evening, passengers gathered around for entertainment such as listening to banjo music. At seventy-nine years of age, Mary became attached to the *Delta Queen* like a barnacle. According to crew members, she still is today.

Many accounts describe a matronly woman, sometimes wearing a green robe and always looking real as roses, walking the ship. Once, when no one was expected on board, one crew member saw a woman striding with purpose down the hallway. He followed her around several corners and into a room. Thinking he had her, he flung the door open. There was no one inside. Concerned the woman was still at large, he reported her to his supervisor. Setting out to find her, they were pulled up short in the hallway by a portrait of Mary Greene. "That's the woman I saw right there," the crewman insisted.

A musician playing on the boat glimpsed a woman in a 1930s dress ambling through the room several times. Each time when she looked up from the keyboard, the woman was gone. Worried the woman was ill or confused, she shared her concerns with a senior crew member, who directed her to the portrait. "That's her," gasped the pianist.

Guests can easily imagine Captain Mary Greene descending the elegant stairway of the Delta Queen.

More than once, tells Matthews, stewards called to deliver food or other goods to a room have found it empty and icy cold. No guests had reserved it. This is most likely to happen in Mary's favorite room, cabin 109. It is also common, says Travis, for guests in 109 to hear knocking in the wall. "We can send the carpenter up there, we can send engineers up there, and they can't find it."

Travis has never seen Captain Greene, but he's heard stories from crew members. Late at night when passengers are asleep or at midday when they have debarked, crew members have seen "a ghostly apparition of a shorter, old woman wandering around . . . midship on the cabin deck," says Travis. She seems to be making her rounds with a quiet confidence, checking that everything's set up correctly for passengers.

Mary can take a very active role when events call for it. One night, Matthews says, a senior crewman felt a kiss on the ear. Or was it a frantic whisper? Was he dreaming? He heard his door slam. Jolted awake, he lurched toward the door, only to hear another door slam down the hall. Now fully awake, heart knocking against his ribs, he followed the sounds until he found himself in the belly of the boat looking at a cracked boiler valve, out of which rushed water. He repaired the valve, saving the *Delta Queen*, and possibly himself, from a watery grave.

Captain Mary's dedication to her boat has piqued the interest of the national media. She and the *Delta Queen* have been featured on *Unsolved Mysteries*, MSNBC, the History Channel's *Haunted History*, and the Travel Channel. Of particular interest is Captain Mary's relationship with the boat's current captain, Michael Williams. Mary seems to have lured him to the old steamer and kept him there.

"I've been working on board almost twenty-five years," says Captain Williams. Starting as a deck hand, he worked his way up by willingly shouldering more responsibility than his crew mates. "My first hitch on the *Delta Queen*, I worked seven months straight. Never went home, never got off the boat. I just loved the idea of being a modern-day Mark Twain, Huck Finn, Tom Sawyer working on an old steamboat."

The *Delta Queen* is more than meets the eye, he explains. "An old wooden boat is a spiritual entity itself because unlike a steel boat, which is cold and lifeless, a wooden boat came from trees that were living things. Over a period of time as it vibrates and travels, it releases some of that energy not only of the people who worked and lived aboard the boat but also the people who built it. I grew to love this old boat, and in return it kinda loved me back."

Despite his strong affection for the *Delta Queen*, he sensed something was missing—the love of a flesh-and-blood soul mate. Living on the boat a month at a time left little opportunity for romance. Williams feared he would have to spurn one true love to find another. But Captain Mary didn't want him to get away. So she played Cupid.

He recalls the night he met Arcadian Cajun Myra Frugé in 1985. "She was an attractive young lady," Captain Williams says, his conviction still strong after more than twenty years. "She had come to work only the week before as a relief purser."

The Louisiana State University public-relations graduate was eager to learn the ropes and make her mark on the *Delta Queen*. One dark night past midnight, as the boat paddled the pulsing waters of the Mississippi, Frugé answered a phone call while working in the purser's office forward.

"It's quiet," remembers Williams. "The boat's trembling gently as we go down the river. No one else is up and around at that hour, the early-morning hours." An elderly lady, her voice weak and trembling, told Frugé she was feeling ill and cold and asked if someone could be sent to help her. The young purser promised to send the mate down to check.

She called the pilothouse and asked Williams, on duty as mate, for help. Williams went straight to cabin 109 and knocked on the door. There was no answer. He knocked again. No answer. Fearing that the woman was unconscious or too ill to reach the door, he used his passkey and opened it. He found the room empty. The beds were neatly made, the packaged mints still on the pillows.

Thinking the new employee had given him the wrong number, he went to the purser's office. "Miss Frugé," he said, "there's nobody in that room. Are you sure she said it was 109?"

She insisted the room number was correct. She told Williams that shortly after she received the appeal for help, she saw "an old lady" looking in the window at her. The woman caught Miss Frugé's eye, smiled slightly, then turned and walked away, making no attempt to talk with her. *Oh my goodness*, Frugé thought, *that's probably the lady who just called.* She hurried out after the lady, who had vanished.

"There was no way she could have got away that fast," says Williams. "We looked on the passenger manifest, and indeed that cabin was not scheduled to have anyone in it. So we thought maybe it was a lady who got her area or location wrong." They decided to keep their eyes open and alert the watchman to look for anyone in need of help. No woman in distress was found.

Later, it occurred to them that there were no telephones in any of the rooms. But Frugé said the elderly woman had phoned.

"She's a real attractive young lady," Williams says again. "She's single and I'm single. I haven't really had much of a chance to talk to this young lady. She'd just come to work here the week before."

So he threw out a line. "You're working late, aren't you?" he said.

She took the bait. "Yeah, but I'm about to wrap it up. I'm tired. I'm going to go down to my cabin."

"I'll walk you down," he offered.

"She lived in the aft crew hold down below," he says. "We walked back silently. We're walking along side by side and talking quietly because we didn't want to disturb anybody. We got right here in front of the pictures [of former *Delta Queen* captains]. She grabbed my arm."

"Hey, wait, stop," she said. "That's the lady I just saw looking at me through the window. Does she work here? Is she one of the managers?"

"I looked at her and realized she didn't know any ghost stories," he says. "She was sincere."

"That couldn't have been her," he told Frugé.

"Oh, yeah, I'm sure that's her. That looks just like her. That's her."

"It couldn't have been," Williams told her. "That's Captain Mary, who died here in 1949."

"Myra's face just went white," Williams says.

"Oh, my God, you're kidding," she said. "Please tell me that's not true. That *was* her that looked in the window, and if it wasn't, it was her twin sister."

Williams had her full attention. "I have some stories to tell you," he said. "Tomorrow, we'll get together when you're off and I'll tell you what's going on."

He walked her down to her cabin. "I didn't get a good-night kiss," he recalls.

As he made his way back to the pilothouse, he paused and looked at the portrait. Captain Mary seemed to be smiling at him.

Romance followed, and the couple wed. They hold dear the memory of their unusual and apparently contrived meeting. Like Williams, Frugé developed a deep fondness for the *Delta Queen*. Immersed in a convivial love triangle, the newlyweds lived together on the boat for almost two years until the birth of their daughter, who has visited the old paddle-wheeler regularly since she was in diapers. Other couples have met and married on board the *Queen* over the years, says Williams.

Crew members continue to attribute any odd occurrences on the boat to Captain Mary. "We've had doors open that were locked, we've had cabinets close, things fall off the shelf when there was obviously nothing vibrating," Travis says. But neither he nor anyone else has ever heard reports of Mary engaging in malicious behavior. Her presence is a friendly one.

Williams says, "You get a feeling like a stern old grandmother who loves you, but she's watching out after you. And if you do something she doesn't like, she'll let you know. And if you do something that she does like, that takes care of her boat, she also takes care of you. I really believe that."

Although a benign spirit, five-foot Mary can be tough. She is dead set against hard liquor and doesn't care who knows it. After her death, someone thought it safe to add a saloon to the ship. Mary expressed her disapproval before the clinking of the first ice cubes. On the first day of the season in about 1953, the bartender stocked the liquor shelves and opened the *Delta Queen*'s new Mark Twain Bar. The boat was loading in Cincinnati for a Mardi Gras cruise to New Orleans, says Travis. Passengers were lining up to board, and the crew was ready for them. Just then, "a tow-boat barge came down through the bridge, lost control, lost its steering, and slammed into the *Delta Queen*," splintering the bar. The name of the wayward barge? The *Captain Mary B.*

But it's a myth that Captain Mary was a teetotaler who didn't allow liquor on her boat, Travis says. In fact, she once toasted her son at a captain's dinner. But she refused to deal in liquor. "Jane Greene [Mary's granddaughter] told me that they did not sell hard liquor because she did not want the Hyde Park Baptist Church to even associate her name with it. Just after Prohibition, there was a big stigma on hard liquor. If you were the person selling it, you were evil."

As for the splintered bar of 1953, the hole was fixed, the bar was opened, and the *Queen* rolled on down the river. A second bar was installed in the old library—now known as the Texas Lounge—without incident.

The Delta Queen docks in Chattanooga at least twice a year.

The timeless *Delta Queen* plows up and down the great American rivers—the Mississippi, the Ohio, and the Tennessee—each year, hostess to hundreds of vacationers. Mary must like Chattanooga because, in late spring and early fall every year, the riverboat docks there. Perhaps she disembarks and strolls the renovated river front, visiting the many ghosts from past centuries said to walk the Scenic City. If she decides to update her wardrobe with a pastel knit pantsuit and some tennis shoes, the plucky captain will blend right in with the hum of the twenty-first-century river town.

the curious case of general grant's headquarters

A house has a soul of its own and, like the souls residing within its walls, desires to love and be loved and to know its place in the order of things. Some houses—like some people—start out full of hope and promise but find, in the end, even friends desert them. Only the ghosts remain, and only because the living believe in them so fervently they are obliged to stay awhile.

Newspaper accounts of the last century described several odd and frightening entities haunting downtown Chattanooga. The most documented was the sad story of the boxy white house at 110 First Street known by generations of Chattanoogans as "General Grant's Headquarters."

The Colonial-style two-story home—the first frame house in Chattanooga—was built in 1838 and by 1848 was the residence of Thomas Lattner and his new bride. In those days, fifty or more rough-hewn cabins dotted the rustic settlement, against which the house stood out like an alabaster jewel box among coarse stones. Perched on a gentle hillside, it was soon hidden among green boughs of pomegranate and other flora thriving under Mrs. Lattner's care. A lavender wisteria vine twined across the front and over the years became a personality in its own right. Gardens carpeted the grounds.

When the War Between the States broke out, Mr. Lattner traveled to Georgia to enlist in the Confederate army. For some time thereafter, the town was festooned with the bright colors of ladies' dresses and men's regimental sashes as citizens made the rounds of dances, picnics, and parties. The war seemed far, far away, and hopes were high.

When the Yankees began shelling Chattanooga in August 1863, young Mrs. Lattner packed her petticoats, chartered a boxcar, and fled to Georgia with her children and "faithful" slaves. The house stood empty and defenseless.

General Ulysses S. Grant rode into Chattanooga on October 23, 1863, flush with victory at the Battle of Vicksburg but still lame from an injury caused by an earlier fall off a horse in New Orleans. That night, Union general George Thomas billeted Grant at the crowded headquarters of General William S. Rosecrans on Walnut Street. Early the next morning, Grant saddled up and set out to find more congenial quarters for himself and the small staff traveling with him.

Just outside the village, Grant came upon the Lattner home. In awe, he reined in his mount and surveyed the structure. He eased down from the horse and, with the help of crutches, hoisted himself up the steps. Legend says he, too, was captivated by the wisteria vine hanging in graceful loops over the doorway.

Before him, the door stood open, as in welcome. Encouraged by this omen, Grant determined to claim the house. He chose a bedroom facing the river for his personal quarters. Before sunset, the walls began their witness to Grant's tactical planning that one month later would pull Chattanooga to its knees and lead to the fall of the Confederacy.

From the Lattner House on First Street in downtown Chattanooga, General U.S. Grant strategized to take the city and crush the Confederacy.
From "Chattanooga Album," courtesy of the Chattanooga-Hamilton County Bicentennial Library

Commanding the house atop the little hill, Grant could survey the field in all directions—Signal Point on Signal Mountain to the northwest, Cameron Hill to the west, Lookout Point on Lookout Mountain to the southwest, the muddy, yellow Tennessee River to the north, and Missionary Ridge to the east.

When the Confederates blockaded the city, food grew scarce for soldiers and civilians alike. Thomas had promised Grant that he and his men would "hold the town until we starve"—and they almost did. Finally, blue-clad troops broke the cordon, and some food slipped in. The Yankees rallied and defeated the Southerners, capturing Orchard Knob, Lookout Mountain, and Missionary Ridge. Grant deserted the war-weary house on November 25 and set up new headquarters at Orchard Knob.

At war's end, the house was stripped of furniture. Part of it had to be demolished. Distressed at its state, benefactors from both North and South put animosity aside and set out to make the house a memorial to fallen soldiers. Patrons placed a bronze tablet at the entrance: "Headquarters, Maj.-Gen. U. S. Grant, U.S.V. Commanding military division of the Mississippi and succeeding Maj. Gen. W. T. Sherman, U.S.V." Legislators introduced bills to make the site a national shrine. Once that battle was lost, the house struggled to reclaim its former beauty and glory. And beneath its crumbling façade lay a more sinister decay. Doomed spirits began to manifest themselves, though no one knows exactly when. Rumors of the hauntings began well before the 1930s.

The first and most persistent revenant to reveal itself was the ghost of a young soldier walking his watch back and forth on the veranda. The sound of steps began at midnight, always moving toward one end, stopping, then returning. Before dawn, they faded away.

The fair-haired boy was fated to walk in death because he had failed his duty in life, sinking into exhaustion and falling into deep slumber at his post. Grant reluctantly ordered him executed, they say. His body was carried off, but his spirit refused to leave. With solitary resolve, he continued to march, proving his allegiance even in death. Over the years, company in the home often heard the sentry's measured tread as he paced outside their windows. Some even claimed to take a certain comfort from the steady steps.

On bleak or chilly nights, guests who found the need to be up and about sometimes saw General Grant himself silently striding the stairs and hallways on his way to bed. Other visitors spied the phantom Grant and Sherman in the parlor, bent over a small table, searching through maps and drawings. Soldiers came and went, bringing and taking reports. The table, maps, and drawings were part of the museum display, the men but fleeting imprints from the past.

Interest in saving the home remained strong through the next decade, even attracting General Grant's grandson to the dedication of the headquarters in 1957. After passing under the wisteria covering the bullet holes that still marred the structure, the young Grant examined the furnishings, pictures, maps, and clocks given by the citizens of Chattanooga.

By the early 1960s, the surrounding community succumbed to urban blight. Vandals marred what little remained of the house. Accounts described it as "gray"— whether in spirit or paint color is unclear.

Spooky entities remained in the old structure. At least three "mystics" were called in to diagnose the problem. One claimed some unseen force stopped her on the steps, keeping her from going up. Another said she saw General Grant three times standing on the front porch as she was leaving. The third said she heard music from stringed instruments playing old Southern songs popular with slaves.

Five years later, the house still gasped for life. Experts deemed it historically and architecturally "insignificant." Attempts to raise twenty-five thousand dollars for restoration were unsuccessful, forcing the Better Housing Authority to condemn it.

Defamed and alone, the house met its end—but not before country singer Johnny Cash saved the flooring, bricks, and other pieces from the wrecking ball. He recycled them into the family chapel on his Middle Tennessee estate. Perhaps there is some chance that, there, the house can regain a small measure of the dignity lost over its last hundred years in Chattanooga.

Today, residents and tourists who walk or jog up the renovated First Street to the nearby Walnut Street Bridge rarely suspect they are retracing the path of Ulysses S. Grant. Does he linger there still? Or did the general and the other ghosts accompany Johnny Cash to his Hendersonville chapel?

IDENTITY CRISIS

As if General Grant's Headquarters had not suffered enough blows, one modern historian now believes the general may *not* have chosen the home as his headquarters. Ever.

Hamilton County historian Patrice Glass theorizes that preservationists and earlier historians believed it to be the headquarters site because it was the only Civil War-era building left downtown and they were reaching for any means to justify its rescue. "People were much more likely to say 'Grant's house' because he became president than they were to say 'Sherman's house' when Sherman had destroyed Georgia," she maintains.

She questions Grant's association with the home. Turning the brittle pages of the *City Atlas of 1889*—the earliest atlas available of Chattanooga—Patrice points to #110 First Street, just off the Walnut Street Bridge to the southwest. "It records it as Sherman's headquarters," she says. Grant's is shown as 316 Walnut. An 1895 guidebook states that Grant headquartered at 110 First Street *and* 316 Walnut Street, about three blocks away. No further details are given. Grant's memoirs don't mention either house.

"Grant may have moved [to the First Street home] once Sherman moved south in the spring," concedes Glass. "The way they moved around so often, it's hard to know exactly in which house he lived the longest. We'll just never know."

Even if 110 First was the spot, the house would have been unrecognizable to the shades of Grant and his sentry in later years. "The house that was saved didn't look anything like it did when he was here," says Patrice.

Please don't tell the ghosts.

read house revenants

CHATTANOOGA, TENNESSEE

Ghosts, it is said, do not have a sense of the temporal. Perhaps that's why some lose all track of hotel checkout times. Or maybe they're just preoccupied. The lively pulse and rich comforts of a grand establishment like the Read House could keep any ghostly guest forever engaged in diverting hotel routines.

The piece of earth over which the Read House now presides did not appear a likely spot for business success in those years just after the Trail of Tears. Eight blocks of near wilderness separated the flood-prone ground from the center of commerce, Ross's Landing, when Thomas Crutchfield began building the first section of a hotel in 1843.

Crutchfield was no fool. He struck an agreement with the Western & Atlantic Railroad. If it would bring tracks and a station, he would construct a hotel, thus benefiting them both and advancing the prospects of the village of Chattanooga.

From a platform in a nearby tree, Crutchfield supervised the labor of family slaves as they framed the three-story landmark that would become known simply as "the hotel." When the railroad arrived in 1851, passengers clomped to the hotel on planks laid at least a foot above the water. One guest later wrote, "In its younger days, your beautiful city was swampy; hence the high planks."

Still, fortune seekers came like bees to a sourwood. In a frontier town of only a few thousand people, the inn became the center of activity. "The hotel swarmed with people arriving and departing with the trains, east, west, north, south, hurrying to and fro with eager and excited looks, as if lives, fortunes, and sacred honor hung upon the events of the next hour," according to Gilbert Govan and James Livingood, quoting a 1857 visitor.

"Rolls of bank notes were exhibited, and net purses with red gold gleaming through their silken meshes," another visitor was overheard to say. "We are in a nest of speculators, where anything may be had at a bargain, ranging from a man's soul down to a beer bottle."

In early 1861, Jefferson Davis, president of the Confederate States of America, stopped overnight at the hotel. After Thomas Crutchfield's brother, William, in the presence of a large audience, denounced Davis as a traitor, the stunned listeners rose to defend their loyalties. Ladies shrieked while men waved pistols. Thomas stepped in and averted bloodshed. Shortly thereafter, sensing the danger posed to business and health by the coming war, he sold the hotel.

Crutchfield's premonition proved true. Confederate troops and refugees poured into the city throughout 1861 and 1862, straining the hotel's modest resources. "Knives and forks were chained to the tables to keep poverty-stricken guests from taking the comforts of home along with them. Brushes and combs were attached to mirror frames, " said one account. The clerks demanded a dollar deposit per towel from each guest.

The hotel served as a Confederate hospital, receiving broken men on trains from the bloody front in Middle Tennessee. Six hundred wounded soldiers packed the rooms and lay on the floors, leaving no place for refugees to stay and overwhelming the small medical staff, including renowned nurse Kate Cummings.

The few citizens left in the city the morning of September 9, 1863, witnessed the Stars and Stripes flapping from the hotel balcony. Days later, many of the Yankees routed at Chickamauga straggled into Chattanooga. Union troops claimed the hotel and filled it with their own wounded. Many men and at least one nurse died there.

When the war ended, the city, or what was left of it, lay treeless and tattered. The hotel had survived the siege but would soon face two more threats. The spring of 1867 brought the greatest flood on record to Chattanooga, sending five feet of muddy water surging through the first floor. The hotel recovered, only to be destroyed by fire that fall.

Construction of a three-story brick office began on the site. But the soul of a hotel remained. In 1871, the Reads took possession and converted the new building into a hotel, again

The 1895 Read House served 200 guests.
Published in *Art Work of Hamilton County.* W.H. Parrish, 1895.

the center of social activity. They added a fourth floor in 1886. Two hundred rooms, including suites, were available. But that was not enough.

New owners demolished most of the brick structure in 1925, leaving the newer north section. They then erected a ten-story section, taking almost the entire block, including the front lawn along the former Ninth Street. Guests could choose from among 414 rooms. It is this footprint that remains today.

It seems some of the guests remain, too. The most legendary is Annalisa Netherly, whose confused and distraught spirit still occupies room 311. Rumors of the tragic Annalisa have circulated throughout the Scenic City for decades.

That she died in the hotel is not up for debate among those who believe in her. But how? Some say she traveled here in the 1920s or 1930s from San Francisco with her husband, who, overcome by jealously at her interest in another, left her here—dead. Others say she committed suicide. And one story pegs her as a lady of the night, killed by a Yankee soldier.

Skeptics can scoff, but too many people have met Annalisa. The women who work at the front desk are often the first to hear the details. "We normally don't rent the room unless it's requested," says reservationist Linda Jenkins. Some guests do request it and may book it years in advance for Halloween.

If the hotel is sold out, the desk staff will rent the finely furnished room. Guests usually don't know the tales of the sad figure who haunts room 311. Linda says, "People who don't have a clue [about the ghost] will come to the front desk in the middle of the night saying, 'I can't tell you what it is, I just can't sleep in there. I need to be moved to another room.' "

Other guests have been more specific about the peculiar goings-on, says Linda. One man left his car keys and change on the dresser in room 311 and returned to find them scattered on the bed.

Children seem more attuned than adults to Annalisa's presence. One mother asked if the hotel was haunted because her little boy said it felt just like their house, also home to a ghost. Another small boy went to the mezzanine restroom while his father waited at the door. He came running out and told his father a woman was inside. She was wearing a long dress and had her hair pulled up. The worried father went straight in. He found no one. Children, says Linda, have discovered the most shocking detail of all about Annalisa. She is pregnant.

Linda thinks she has come into contact with the ghost. Guests at a December wedding asked if they could see the infamous room. Finding it vacant, Linda took the group of about eight people up. One person videotaped the visit while Linda, the good hostess, stood by the door so the visitors could explore the room. "All the sudden, there's a loud knocking on the door. I'm standing right beside the door. I opened it, thinking another friend wanted to come and see. There was nobody there. So I stepped out into the hall." Linda didn't see anyone, and there was nowhere to hide. The knocker had vanished. Wondering if their imaginations had run away with them, they played the video back. "You hear the loud knocking at the door and you hear the door open, and there's nobody there."

Employee Howard Johnson has encountered Annalisa, too. He has worked in the hotel for forty-six years. When asked point-blank if there is a ghost within, he says without pause, "There is."

But for more than thirty years, he didn't believe the stories he heard about Annalisa. He had to see her for himself. One fall in the late 1990s, he was upstairs in room 311 watching football on television. "Tennessee was playing Alabama. I was sitting on the bed, and this lady come from nowhere. I went to the door and asked could I help her, and she wouldn't say nothin'. So I thought maybe she wanted to come in and ask me

Porter Howard Johnson will not enter Read House room 311 unless forced to.

what the score was." Since she refused to say one word to him, Howard called the front desk and told the clerk that an unidentified woman stood at the door, apparently in need of assistance. "By the time I went to the door, she disappeared."

The woman seemed as real as the opulent hallway surrounding her. "She was a blond-headed lady, real pretty. She had an evening gown on."

Howard says the staring woman wasn't frightening. Her peculiar behavior simply baffled him. "I didn't know what the problem was. She just pop up on me from nowhere. I don't believe in stuff like that. But I saw her myself. Real pretty lady, real pretty lady."

Leaving the door open, Howard went downstairs and recruited the hotel engineer to help. "We get back upstairs, and the door's shut. So we went to stick the key in the room, and she wouldn't even let us open the door."

Annalisa is persnickety about her privacy, sometimes refusing entry to guests, especially men. Is the lock on room 311 defective? "The lock is fine," Howard says.

When she does allow people in, their stay may not be a peaceful one. "We have guests say they can't sleep all night.

They hear water running. One guest said she saw the lady standing over the bed." And Annalisa doesn't like cigarette smoke. "If you light a cigarette, she'll put it out," Howard warns.

"All kinds of things happen. Everybody has a different story. Mirrors fall off the wall in room 311, and lights go out when people come in. One person said they were sitting in there. The next thing you know, the TV went off. Every time they cut it back on, when they getting ready to set down, it go right back off."

It's not just a solitary person alone in the room who experiences the revenant. Annalisa is not shy around groups. A television crew came in, says Howard. "They couldn't shoot the picture. She wouldn't let 'em. Every time they'd try to take the picture, the cameras just fall."

One group of guests refused to sleep on the third floor, having come face to face with the roaming Annalisa. They camped out in the lobby. This has happened more than once, Howard says. She doesn't limit herself to the third floor. Some guests have seen her—or other entities—elsewhere, including the fourth, fifth, sixth, and seventh floors.

Since his own encounter with the ghost, Howard admits he makes every effort to avoid entering room 311, even to help a guest, including one woman who found herself all soaped up in the shower when the water suddenly stopped. The hotel offered her the use of another room.

Howard arrived and stood in the doorway. She asked if he was going to carry her bags. He didn't budge. "Ma'am," he said, "you're not leaving the room until the engineer come, and we're going to let you take a shower in another room."

"That's nice of you," she said, likely perplexed at why an engineer was required to move her. "Could you come in and help me get these?" she asked again, referring to her bags in the back of the room.

Howard tried to stall. "Are you dressed, ma'am?"

"I have my housecoat on."

Howard finally relented, lest he appear totally lacking in hospitality. He almost tripped over a chair as he went about his duties.

He will show the room to curious visitors but always keeps one foot in the hall. "I don't think she'd hurt nobody. The problem is you're hurting yourself," he says, chuckling.

Annalisa doesn't much like men, says Howard, pursing his lips and refusing to speculate further. Her opinion of them has not improved over the years. There are tales of men leaving half naked in the middle of the night to escape the gaze of Annalisa. One man, hearing of the ghost, refused to even check in, asking the driver to take him to another hotel.

Al Capone sure doesn't seem the sort she would care to associate with. If the gangster tangled with her during his stay in room 311 in the early 1930s, he didn't say. Perhaps he came and went before Annalisa checked in. Rumors also circulate that Elvis once stayed at the hotel, seeking some rest and recreation. But there have been no recorded sightings of him, dead or alive.

The dejected young woman does not roam the hotel alone. Because it was a hospital during the Civil War, investigators believe its halls and rooms—especially the basement, which served as the hospital morgue—may harbor other supernatural energies. "We've had ghost busters from California, from all over, come and stay here. They say they really do get high readings," Linda says.

Everyone at the Read House seems to know about these long-term guests. Some of them, such as former food and beverage manager Natalie Kelly, wish they didn't. She tries hard to disregard the tales. "You hear everybody talk about all these superstitions," she says dismissively. Yet even Natalie admits there's something just a little bit creepy lurking in the hidden corners of the building late at night—indistinct noises and formless shadows. These she would refuse to investigate.

She would hurry in, get the job done, and dash out.

Initially closed-lipped about the details—"We don't volunteer information," she says—Natalie is eventually coaxed into revealing her own piece of the paranormal puzzle. Her first week at the Read House, the elevator stopped. She summoned help. "They called the car down to the basement and got me out. Another time, I got in the elevator just to go to the basement. All the lights lit up, and it just stopped." *Don't freak out, it'll be okay. You're a big girl*, she said to herself. "It started going down and stopped midway between the lobby level and the basement level. Then all of a sudden, it shot me up rather quickly, and it opened up at the fourth floor." She ran out of the elevator and encountered a waiting guest in business attire. Before he could step through the doors, she grabbed him and, telling him the elevator was out of order, made off with him down three flights of stairs.

Still, she attempts a rational explanation. "It's an old building. Things do happen."

Perhaps the building's age does account for the elevator with a mind of its own, the flickering lights during the October 2004 renovation, the nonworking showers, and the other odd occurrences over many years. Nonetheless, the staff at the Read House take their celebrated guest quite seriously and strive to keep her comfortable.

"Because Annalisa doesn't like smoke," says Linda, "we changed the smoking floor from the third to the fifth floor."

And, adds Linda, room 311 is one of the best appointed in the hotel.

How fortunate, for Annalisa appreciates the finer things in life . . . and death.

The University of Tennessee at Chattanooga's Hooper Hall off McCallie Avenue, circa 1920.
Courtesy of Lupton Library Special Collections, University of Tennessee at Chattanooga

haunted hooper hall

CHATTANOOGA, TENNESSEE

Any college worth its ivy is haunted. The venerable University of Tennessee at Chattanooga's history is long and rich and sometimes tragic. The campus on the hilltop has been the scene of several sorrows of the sort that invite ghosts. Surely, the saddest of these was the man who took his own life in a futile effort to join loved ones in death.

At least one enigmatic, unseen entity paces the floors of Hooper Hall, a UTC administrative building overlooking McCallie Avenue. Professors, staff, and students often hear heels click-clacking down the hall, going one direction, then turning and coming back.

Administrator Sandy Cole encountered the ghost one night in the early 1980s. Snow and sleet were pelting the city, blanketing the university's sidewalks and parking lots. Sandy's then-husband, Bob Mills, was responsible for readying the campus for class the next day. So the two of them packed their sleeping bags and a change of clothes and set up a sofa bed in the Admissions Office on the first floor.

The building had been locked up by security, as usual. The office doors had windows in them, but Sandy was unconcerned about privacy, since no one else was there. Or so she believed. They settled in at midnight or shortly thereafter. Before they fell asleep, a door slammed somewhere in the building. Then they heard footsteps outside their door. *Lord,* thought Sandy, *who would be in this building this time of night?* "It kept walking, walking, walking, walking," she says. "You could hear it. On the first floor."

Bob got up to look. "He didn't see a soul anywhere, and the noise stopped," Sandy remembers.

"I swear I heard something," she told him when he came back.

Bob assured her he had heard it, too. But since he had found no sign of an intruder, he fell back into bed.

Once more, a door slammed. Then came more footsteps. Bob looked again. Nothing. "I didn't sleep another minute that night," he later told a reporter for the student paper, the *University Echo.*

Sandy, who had never heard the tales of a ghost roaming Hooper Hall, was frightened that a strange person might have entered the building. Clad in pajamas near an uncovered door window into the hallway, she felt vulnerable. But since there was nothing to do but try to get some rest, they settled back in.

At about three or four in the morning, they heard a clock cuckooing in the dean's office. "I didn't think anything about that," she says. But it did interfere with a good night's sleep.

The next morning, a weary Sandy mentioned the clock to the dean's secretary. The secretary told her the clock did not cuckoo. Sandy was taken aback. The clock had never cuckooed before, she was told—and it hasn't since.

Bob began to ask around about the curious events. Security personnel told him they had investigated muddy footprints in the building one evening. Strangely, the footprints led nowhere. They went so far, then simply disappeared. "I would never spend another night in that building again. . . . There is definitely *something* in that building," Bob told the *Echo*.

Custodians have heard wheezing coming from the first-floor front hallway and noises similar to furniture moving and doors slamming on the second floor. Another active area is the floor directly over the vending machines, which sit between the two main hallways of the first floor. The elevator has been known to ascend to the top floor as if summoned by an invisible passenger. The upper stairwell once dropped in temperature so far and fast that the person unfortunate enough to be coming down alone saw her breath turn frosty. A malevolent and aggressive entity has been sensed in the stairwell. Yet when these puzzling events occur, no one else is in the building, which is almost always locked up and dark.

Students braving overnight campouts in Hooper Hall in hopes of meeting the ghost have documented cold spots three to four feet in diameter and witnessed outside lights going on and off. There are also rumors of a bloodlike dampness seeping from the walls.

Chuck Cantrell, assistant vice chancellor of university relations, set out to explain the strange happenings in Hooper. A psychic, working from only a piece of paper with "615 McCallie Avenue" scribbled on it, told Chuck the ghost is that of a man named John. He couldn't see John's face but felt he had hanged himself in the building in an area containing chemicals.

A subsequent search through old city newspapers revealed a startling account of heartache and anguish. Fifty-year-old John Hockings, the university's superintendent of grounds and buildings, had committed suicide in the physics laboratory two weeks after Christmas 1923, at seven o'clock in the morning on January 7, 1924. In those years, Hooper Hall was the science building. But rather than hanging himself, as the psychic suggested, Hockings had rigged up gas piped through a rubber hose. When his body was discovered in the lab, his face was obscured by a quilt, possibly all he had left of his beloved wife, who, with their only child, had died some years earlier in a fire.

The native of England was described as conscientious and hardworking. He had arrived on campus by four o'clock each morning to light the heating-plant fires. The *University Echo* eulogized him as "a loyal and faithful supporter of the college at all times."

Nineteen years before his death, Hockings had enrolled in the university to prepare for the ministry. Soon thereafter, grieving over his family, he lost heart and dropped out. Nonetheless, Hockings remained as an employee and seems to have embraced every social activity available, possibly in an effort to ease his loneliness. He joined almost ten organizations, including First Methodist Episcopal Church. The entire student body attended his funeral in Patten Chapel. According to the university, Hockings had been "very despondent at times" since his family's death. But because he left no note, "so far as was discovered, . . . there was no reason for his action." Seen but not heard, his life ended in lonely despair.

If he desired to reunite with his wife and child in death, he may have failed. His trapped spirit is believed to still pace the halls after dark.

A Study of Ghosts

Ghosts are also thought to haunt UTC's Brock Hall, Patten Chapel, Development House, and Lambda Chi House. Chuck Cantrell's curiosity about the stories of UTC's disquieted spirits led him to question Dr. William G. Roll, professor of psychology and psychical research at West Georgia College, now the University of West Georgia. Roll explained that some ghost stories really are the fruit of overactive imaginations or substance abuse. Others cannot be explained.

After consulting with Roll, Cantrell theorized none of UTC's ghosts are malicious. They are attracted to the camaraderie shared by students. Or they may be former employees who were happy during their tenures at the school.

"No one is really scared of them," he insists. "The stories are passed around campus in the form of water-fountain chuckles among faculty and staff. And besides, nobody wants to go on record as having seen or heard a ghost."

That includes Cantrell. "I came up at night to see for myself. I didn't find any," he says.

Or they didn't find him.

little margie

CHATTANOOGA, TENNESSEE

Ghosts, especially those of children, seem bound to the places that sheltered them in the flesh, even if such lives were cruel or horribly ended. This small spirit, left behind and maybe alone, must have gleefully greeted the opening of a popular dining establishment in her "home." While the night is young, fun and fellowship prevail. But when the revelers go home, the dark loneliness closes in. What happens when the revelers never return?

The rambling old house at 3819 Brainerd Road spent decades as a residence in the popular suburb of Brainerd before opening its doors to diners as an unusual but very popular Ruby Tuesday restaurant. A hodgepodge of tacked-on rooms and enclosed porches, the one-story maze of a house didn't seem a likely candidate for an eating establishment. It certainly wasn't like other Ruby Tuesdays, which, like all chain stores, can be counted on to offer a certain décor and ambiance wherever they might be. But Chattanoogans flocked to the old house to eat, drink, and socialize.

Unknown to most diners, an unseen someone mingled among the crowds of the living. Although they kept it to themselves, the staff knew that no matter how many guests might be in the restaurant, an invisible prankster was there, too, hiding and waiting. And they didn't want to meet up with her alone. Waitresses would not travel to the basement ice machine unless accompanied by another living, breathing human being. They were scared.

"No one goes down there by themselves. No way!" said manager Tommy Janney during a 1989 interview.

"That stairway is where a child fell and was killed," says former waitress Nicole Kotarski Newcom. "The door would always slam shut by itself."

To avoid finding themselves trapped at the bottom alone, nervous waitresses scurried down the stairway in pairs. When that led to the loss of precious time—and income—management moved the ice machine to the main floor.

All seemed safe as long as diners and drinkers were congregating and the hour was early. But late at night, the basement's mischievous little spirit, known as "Little Margie" by local ghost hunters, would come upstairs to play. She delighted in turning the TV on and off and pushing a Bud Lite advertising display bottle off the shelf.

The lights often went out for no obvious reason. Nicole tells about one of the regulars who sat at the bar every night with his drink and keys before him. One time, the man was slouching in his usual spot at almost one-thirty in the morning when, without warning, the lights went out. Even with the hard glimmer of the emergency lights, it was still dark. But not so dark a person wouldn't notice movement just inches away, right in front of his eyes.

When the power came back on, the man's keys were gone.

He looked around him. "Hey! Who took my keys?" He hadn't seen anyone move toward him, nor had he heard the jingling of keys nearby. He accused his drinking buddies and the restaurant's employees of playing a joke. No one came forward with the keys. A search turned up nothing. He never saw his keys again.

One evening when Janney and his fiancée went to the second floor to close up, they heard the odd noises common in the restaurant during the 1980s. It sounded like keys rattling on the copper-topped bar. Then two heavy footsteps fell on the hardwood floor. Next, paper rustled behind the bar—where there was no paper! Janney, concerned an intruder stalked the restaurant, picked up a pole and "walked around, knowing it wouldn't do anything to a ghost." He found nothing—no keys, no intruder, no one.

Because of these unexplained phenomena, it was against company policy for anyone to stay in the restaurant alone after closing.

"It was always creepy at night when you had to close," says Nicole. "Nobody ever liked to go back in the kitchen by themselves."

One evening, Nicole, known among her friends as a fearless adventurer, volunteered to check the kitchen. As she started back, she heard what sounded like metal hitting the floor. Thinking she needed to pick up whatever had fallen, she entered the area where, each night before going home, the cooks slipped spatulas into a slot on the back of the grill. When Nicole reached the grill, she saw a spatula flip into the air, then crash to the floor. Two were already on the floor—probably the source of the clatter that drew her there. "People would find spatulas on the floor all the time," she says.

Before leaving, the late crew would turn off the lights, televisions, and computers and lock every door. "The next morning," says Nicole, "the doors would be open, everything would be turned on, and nobody would be in there. That happened a lot. Managers were getting in trouble all the time. But nothing was ever taken—it wasn't a break-in."

The sad sounds of a small child crying sometimes spooked conscientious employees. They would race to help the fretful baby but find no one. One manager of the restaurant became so intrigued with the ghost, rumored to be the spirit of a murdered two-year-old, that he hired a security company to hook up a listening device in the restaurant, to be monitored from the police station.

According to Jamie Smith, once a corporate trainer for Ruby Tuesday, the police called a manager at two o'clock in the morning and told him they believed someone had left a baby in the restaurant, since they heard crying through the security system. The manager hurried over to rescue the abandoned infant but found the place completely empty. Later that night, the police called again. He searched the building once more and found no one.

The ghost's identity and cause of death are matters of speculation. Employees shared stories, no doubt changing them a little in each recounting. But all rumors involved the basement.

Death by falling down the stairs is plausible. Another story says a mother murdered her child in the basement, burned her in the fireplace, then buried her ashes and bones under the hearth. The child was said to be handicapped. Some believe she was murdered out of compassion. The Depression had resulted in total ruin for her once-affluent family, who were unable to feed her. So speculation about the motive ranges from mercy to insanity.

Is there any truth to the gruesome tales of murder by fire? The four-thousand-square-foot house was believed to have been built in 1920. Thus, it stood during the Depression. But no one knows for certain if any child ever died in the house or if the family living there during the Depression suffered financial collapse. A small newspaper item reported the burning death of a local two-year-old in 1920, but no name was given. Deemed accidental, the death was said to have been caused by standing too close to an open fireplace. Ghastly deaths by fire were commonly reported in the early years of the twentieth century. It is impossible to say if the child in the 1920 article ever lived in the house. At that time, obituaries were published only for "important" people.

So who—or what—generated the heavy footsteps at the restaurant? The child's murderer? A guilty father? A former patron attracted to alcohol and levity from beyond the grave?

The strange happenings go back many years. Nicole remembers her grandmother Katy talking about visiting the home long before it became a restaurant. The residents thought the place held secrets even then. The eerie experiences continued for years. "Sometimes, it would just get hair-raising," concluded corporate trainer Smith. "There's no doubt in my mind there's a ghost."

Did the ghost doom the vintage house? The restaurant moved out in 1992 and relocated to a local mall, where it continues to serve up food and spirits—of the alcoholic sort only. Despite its apparent structural soundness and good location, the house attracted no tenants for four years. Sentenced to the wrecking ball, it is no more. Today, the site where the restaurant once stood is a sloping, roughly paved lot whose emptiness is made more naked by the buzz of commerce surrounding it.

Where did Little Margie go? Not far, apparently. Just down the hill at 3709 Brainerd Road, within walking distance even for a toddler, another old house sits. No doubt, it is one that Margie visited in the days when neighbors spent time together. It could even be that this vintage building, now a window and siding business, was Margie's home, and that the old Ruby Tuesday was just an irresistible temptation to a sociable rascal.

The former residence turned business at 3709 Brainerd Road may be the current stomping ground of Little Margie.

Like Ruby Tuesday, the house at 3709 Brainerd Road fell on hard times. In the last two decades, several tenants came and went, two nightclubs among them. During that time, the house suffered its second fire. It survived but was close to condemnation when businessman Mike Stewart bought it. Stewart completely gutted the structure before remodeling it to suit his window business. A strange feeling came over him when he tore the ceiling out in the basement and discovered an old fireplace and, around it, evidence of an earlier fire. Later, an elderly man told Stewart he had grown up nearby and played with one of the children who had lived in the house. He remembered that a baby had died in the basement, burned to death.

Did Margie die here, rather than in the old Ruby Tuesday? Or did two children meet death in basement fireplaces in the same neighborhood?

Someone haunts Stewart's building. But who?

Almost immediately, Stewart noticed the basement stayed at a constant, moderate temperature except for one back room. It's freezing in there, he says. A person exhales frosty breath. "That let me know there was a spirit or something there."

He had heard about the Ruby Tuesday ghost since his high-school years in the mid-1970s. Everybody at Howard

High School and the whole community seemed to know about it—and some wished they didn't. There seemed to be a sense that the lost baby was still around.

During the remodeling, Stewart called the police when he discovered a break-in. An officer came and waited outside. Stewart suggested he go in and see the shattered window where the burglar had entered.

"I don't need to see it," the officer replied.

"Don't you need to make a report?"

"No. I don't want to go into that building," the officer said.

Baffled, Stewart asked why.

"I don't know if you know it or not, but that building's haunted."

"You're joking, right?"

"I'm not joking, and I don't want to go in there. We've had a lot of reports on that building. That building's haunted."

The haunting has never bothered Stewart. He was born with a "veil," or caul, over his face—evidence, his parents told him, that he could see spirits. He has seen several. A baby ghost was not going to stop him from enjoying a prime piece of Chattanooga real estate. He finished the renovation and moved in. Two years later, he tells his own ghost stories.

Often, working at one and two o'clock in the morning, he notices the sound of footsteps in the attic. One evening, worried that a dog or other large animal was trapped there, he searched for it with a flashlight but saw nothing. Still, signs of the entity greet him some mornings. He finds his credenza, cleaned the evening before, sprinkled with thick dust that has fallen from the ceiling during the night, as if shaken loose.

And the phones have acted peculiar. At first, he didn't say anything, not wanting to frighten the office staff. But after a few late nights, they came to him and reported the phone problems. Lines two and three lit up as if someone had activated them. But no one else was there. When a blinking line was picked up, only static could be heard. Thinking his new phones were defective, Stewart insisted the vendor replace the entire system. Still, the lights blinked randomly, always after midnight. He has called service men several times to check the phones and new lines. Nothing is wrong, they all tell him.

He knows it's the ghost. She seems to be playing a game with him. If he looks at a blinking phone, it stops. When he looks away, it flickers again. Determined to find which office houses the phone responsible for the blinking lines, he rushes from office to office some nights. But the blinking always stops before he can solve the mystery. His staff is terrified.

Despite his ability to see spirits, Stewart has yet to witness one at his place of business. But he believes ghosts choose to reveal themselves. Maybe one evening he will see whoever is working a shadowy third shift, making stomping sounds and causing the phones to blink. Will it be Little Margie?

the ghost who typed "Boo"

EAST RIDGE, TENNESSEE

Signal Mountain resident Janice Hayes is in her forties but has about her the sense of adventure and sparkle of a young girl. That's most likely why she was befriended by the most playful ghost in town—Irving.

Back in the mid-1990s, when Janice Hayes was a married woman, her in-laws lived in a ranch house in East Ridge, as did a friendly spirit they called Irving. It wasn't long before Janice was initiated into the family secret.

"Once, we were all sitting around the table," says Janice, "and there was a Christmas decoration that you had to plug in the wall, flip a switch, and then Santa Claus would start to sing or something. Well, it wasn't plugged in. Nobody reached over and flipped it on. But all of a sudden, it started."

Janice thought this very peculiar, and she wasn't sure what could have caused it. But her mother-in-law knew very well, since she had interacted with Irving quite regularly for years.

After her two boys were grown and gone, she would often be alone in bed at night when her husband traveled. She'd hear somebody walking around the house—not causing any trouble, just walking. She knew as sure as she knew her own breathing that it was Irving.

Once, when Janice's in-laws were in bed, somebody grabbed her mother-in-law's hand. She said to her husband, "You're squeezing my hand too tight."

He rolled toward her. "Both hands are right here. What are you talking about?"

She didn't worry too much about that. It was just Irving, in need of a little reassurance.

But Janice, still new to the family, remained a tad skeptical about Irving. So Irving took it in good humor and endeavored to win her attention. He showed up at her downtown office one day with a plan.

"We have computers, but we also have electric typewriters," says Janice. "I was working on my computer. My typewriter was plugged in, but it was turned off. All of a sudden, it just starts typing away. Typing madly away. I thought, *What on earth?* So I got a piece of paper and stuck it in. It was just typing. I don't type that fast. It was like eighty words per minute, *very* fast. The keys were moving. It just typed and typed and typed. And then it stopped.

"I pulled the piece of paper out, and the whole page was covered with symbols that I didn't even know my typewriter had. There was a pound sterling symbol on there. There were weird things. But right in the middle of all this nothing—no words, just a jumble of symbols and figures and stuff—there was one word: *Boo.* That's all it said.

"I thought, *That's Irving just welcoming me to the family, just saying hi.*"

Janice, astounded and delighted, tucked the message away in a safe place at home as evidence to anyone, including herself, that it had really happened.

When she and her husband decided to divorce, Irving showed up at their house, where they still lived together amicably. Perhaps Irving thought a little levity was called for during that sad time.

Janice's soon-to-be ex-husband always went to work earlier than she did, leaving her alone in the house for a short time. She didn't think about ghosts in the morning. Like most Americans, she raced the clock to get out the door.

"I had a stack of clothes on my dresser. Some of them had fallen on the floor, and one was this real bright red pair of panties. You couldn't miss it," says Janice. "Normally, I would have picked them up and thrown them in the laundry basket. But that morning, I was running late and in a hurry." So Janice rushed through her morning routine. She didn't notice Irving had let himself in.

"We had several cats," she says. "Lance, the big orange cat, was in the bedroom walking around. Before I went into the bathroom, he hopped up on the bed and was peacefully lying there."

Janice went into the bathroom to get ready. Ten minutes later, she was made up and ready to leave for work. She passed through the bedroom, where Lance was still curled on the bed, asleep.

"I stopped dead in my tracks. There's that bright red pair of panties—you couldn't miss it because of the color—and it was neatly folded and lying on the cat. I called my husband and said, 'Hey, you didn't come back for anything, did you?'"

Her husband told her no and wondered why she even asked. On hearing about the covered cat, he suggested that the more energetic cats might have picked up the panties and carried them around.

Janice didn't buy it. "I would understand if the underwear was up on the bed or even thrown over his back. But it was folded more neatly than I fold. [Lance] was still sound asleep. He wouldn't have been if the other cats had been romping about. I fully believe it was Irving come to say good-bye to me," she says.

Janice and her ex-in-laws don't know for sure who Irving is. Or was. But he's been an active member of the family for some time. Janice's ex-husband told her he'd even experienced Irving growing up. "He'd spend the nights with friends, and Irving would come along and do weird things," Janice says.

Before her in-laws moved into the house, built in the early 1950s, there was an incident with a developmentally challenged young man, she says. "He may have not been killed there but died there—maybe in the fifties or sixties—and they think it might be him. There were just too many things that happened in that house for them to put it down to the house creaking or shifting or moving or atmospheric changes or weather."

Janice believes in Irving now, but she's not the least bit spooked. She even claims to miss him. "Irving for the most part was a nice spirit." Besides, she says, "ghosts don't scare me. They can't hurt me. I'm a Christian."

Irving doesn't want to hurt anyone. But a goose bump or two is not out of the question.

night drummers

LOOKOUT MOUNTAIN, TENNESSEE

Civil War reenactments are popular in the South. Men act out the courageous deeds of other men long gone to honor and remember them. But sometimes, soldiers on the field are not actors. They are shadows and echoes of the very troops who fought and died there, struggling through battle one more time.

Musicians seem to prefer quaint and quirky places to live. You rarely see them in Masonite-sided apartment buildings or brick duplexes in the suburbs. So when the group Overland Express found an old house on the side of Lookout Mountain about a hundred yards below the Cravens House on Shingle Road, the members moved in.

It was some the worse for wear, as vintage homes often are. The load-bearing wall down the middle of the house had settled, which caused some aggravation. "An old-fashioned kitchen pantry depended on that long wall," explains band member Rick Williams. "The house had settled so hard we could not get that door open. We even took the hinges off." But the two-story house was spacious, well crafted, and close to downtown Chattanooga, so the new tenants gave up on the pantry door and made themselves at home.

In those years, the early 1980s, the band spent many long hours on the road touring with Gregg Allman and usually fell into bed upon getting back. One night, the members made it home early enough to rehearse before turning in. "We were picking acoustics and started hearing drums, like field drums," Rick says. "It wasn't one—it was a lot of them. We'd stop. 'Do you hear that?' 'Not really.' 'It's something, but I don't know what.' Then we could hear people talk outside. Surely, somebody's out in our yard. So we walked outside on the back porch. Not a soul out there."

The men thought it very unlikely anyone could have come up the steep and rugged hill toward their house in the dark. And who would want to? Still, they trudged outside to investigate. "It was foggy and cold, but we sat there until about two in the morning. We couldn't hear anything. So we went back in the house, and we could hear people talking, mumbling, still drumming."

Nothing could be done for it, so Rick went to his bedroom and settled in with a book. "As I lay in the bed, the noise got

As the night deepened on the side of Lookout Mountain, the drums beat louder and louder.

louder and louder and louder. Every now and then, it sounded like someone would scream an order. It got to the point that it was so loud it was about to scare me." At four or five in the morning, the house should have been dead quiet. The television, radios, and stereos were all off. Yet the mysterious noise filled the night. "It got so loud I opened my door to look out in the hall. Keith was standing there looking at me, and Michael was standing there looking at Keith, then they both looked at me."

"Something's going on outside," Mike said.

"Did you hear it, Keith?" Rick asked.

"Yeah, I heard it. I couldn't help but hear it, it was so loud."

"I had cold chills," says Rick. "I didn't know what was going on. Keith didn't either. Keith's a Vietnam vet."

As daybreak drew near, the three men huddled in Keith's room. Left by a former roommate, a poster commemorating the 1863 "Battle Above the Clouds" leaned haphazardly atop a stack of boxes in the corner. "Look!" one of the men said, pointing at the date on the poster. "What's today's date?" All three realized the question was loaded. The battle took place November 24 through the early hours of November 25, which happened to be the current date.

The fame of the battle surpasses its substance. Union general Ulysses S. Grant is reputed to have said, "The battle of Lookout Mountain is one of the romances of the War. There was no action worthy to be called a battle on Lookout Mountain; it is all poetry." But for the men who fought and died there, the experience carried deep meaning. Still, Grant can't be blamed for hinting at the poetic splendor of the landscape that night.

The scene was an eerie one. On the morning of November 24, 1863, the fog enshrouding the top of the mountain and rolling down its eastern and northeastern lower slopes was so thick that some troops struggled to see the enemy and each other. During the day, a light drizzle gave rise to a cold gloom. But Grant, desperate to shatter the Rebels' grip on Chattanooga, ordered General Joseph Hooker to keep the defenders distracted while Sherman launched the Union attack on Missionary Ridge.

Ten thousand Confederates were scattered across the high ground, some too distant to effectively defend against the attack. Sharpshooters and a cannon battery were in place at the summit. Some troops defended the "bench" below the bluffs, located near the Cravens House and around the northwestern slope. When they couldn't see the Yankees, they fired at the flashes of their guns in the hope they might hit the soldiers holding them. Confederate general John Brown had his men roll rocks down the mountain, possibly as much to terrify the enemy solders as to crush them.

The fog helped the Union forces surprise General Edward Walthall's fifteen hundred Mississippians, who couldn't see ten thousand blue boys trudging up the slopes. The Cravens House fell into the hands of Union general W. C. Whitaker, who made it his headquarters. By midafternoon, much of the fighting had ended. Nearly half of Walthall's brigade had been captured.

Yankee troops struggled to see the action from their posts in Chattanooga. The fog cleared at dusk, revealing "the parallel fires of the two armies, extending from the summit of the mountain to its base, looking like streams of lava, while in between, the flashes from the skirmishers' muskets glowed like fireflies," according to Union general Joseph Fullerton. Yet there seemed little hope the Yankees could wrest the stronghold from the entrenched Rebels.

Gunfire continued through the night. "A full moon made the battlefield as plain to us in the valley as if it were day," reported Union assistant secretary of war Charles Dana. Shortly after midnight, Peter Cozzens wrote, the moon's "brilliant beams glittered on the icy rocks and cast weird shadows in the deep crevices." Just after two o'clock in the morning, the moon went into eclipse, fading to a deep red and casting a pall over the mountainside. Viewing the blood moon as an ominous sign, the Confederates used it to cloak their flight to Missionary Ridge, where defeat awaited them.

Union troops scaling the bluffs the next morning were startled to find the defenders gone. Confederate losses were 125 killed, 300 wounded and left on the field, and 1,054 captured or missing. Federal casualties numbered 480. As for the Cravens House, only a charred frame and chimneys survived the battle and the scavenging for materials that followed.

Rick and his roommates were stunned at the realization that the very ground on which soldiers died during the legendary battle was that beneath their feet. "We really got goose bumps," says Rick. "When we looked at the dates on that poster, I don't think anybody said a word for about fifteen minutes. We just stood there and stared at it."

Rick broke the silence. "Do you know what we just experienced? A reenactment of what happened a hundred years ago, guys. That's what was going on here, whether you believe it or not. But I believe it."

At dawn, the drumbeats retreated.

When they had first moved in, Rick didn't feel negative energy in the house. Even the long roll of the ghostly drummers didn't alarm him unduly. But as the months passed, he began to feel more and more ill at ease.

The ranger stationed at Chickamauga and Chattanooga National Military Park told the men the battle was not the only occasion for violent death there. Someone had been murdered in the house where they were living. Who, why, and how remain a mystery. Whatever happened had left the house with restless psychic energy. Something just wasn't right.

One brittle February evening, the men returned home late after a gig. Although one roommate had stayed home, the guys didn't hold out much hope he had stoked the coal furnace in the basement. "He . . . never helped us do dishes or anything," says Rick. Tired and cold, they dreaded making the trip to the dark basement to shovel coal. To their surprise, when they opened the front door, they found it toasty warm inside.

Rick felt remorse for badmouthing his housemate. "I took back everything I said about him because he did go down there and do that. I said, 'I take it back, buddy. You went down there and stoked up the furnace.' "

"I didn't do it," the housemate said.

"You're the only one who's been here all night."

"I didn't do it."

Curious, Rick and Mike descended the stairs with a flashlight and found the furnace at full blaze. They figured it had burned six to eight hours and should have settled to warm ashes. "Cool, somebody likes us," Rick muttered to himself.

"But then everything got weird," he recalls. "We came home one night and there was some stuff off the dinner table that was broken. The house had been empty all day. So we looked for signs of somebody breaking in and [found] nothing—the doors were locked, our guitars and amps were still there. Later that week, we played, came home, and went to bed. Then there was this awful noise downstairs—a loud, glass-breaking noise. It scared Michael so bad he got his shotgun. We just knew somebody was in the house."

The men trooped downstairs together and found the once-unyielding pantry door standing wide open. "There were fifteen to twenty old jam and jelly jars that someone had thrown off the kitchen wall and busted," Rick says. "We were all barefooted, and there was glass and grape jelly all over the place."

After the jelly-jar attack, the men decided "it was too crazy to live there."

"I felt like we weren't wanted," says Rick. He told Keith and Michael, "I'm not a man of violence. I don't like to be around it. I'm getting out tomorrow."

True to his word, he left the following morning.

tales from northwest
georgia

blades and roses

FLINTSTONE, GEORGIA

Just looking upon this house can pull people to it or warn them away. For those chosen by the house, to enter its domain is to fall under a sweet and dreamy spell. For those not welcomed, it is best to get out. But no real evil lurks there—just some protective spirits, themselves seduced by the home's hypnotic magic decades ago.

"I remember riding up that driveway as a child, maybe about ten years old," says Thom Calvin about the old Grant House in Blowing Springs, at the foot of Lookout Mountain in Chattanooga Valley. He often came along when his father hayed the nearby fields. Thom had plenty of time of the sort children used to spend imagining and speculating.

"The house had been vacant for who knows how many years. And it looked very spooky. It was a dingy white with blacked-out shiny windows of lead-filled glass. From the outside looking in, it looked black—the reflection was toward you, and nothing inward. I wouldn't ride up there around the circle, just up to the bottom of it. At that time, it had a different vibe to it."

But Thom was drawn back to the house almost twenty years later. In 1984, it became his home. It had just been featured by the Chattanooga Symphony as a Decorator Show House. The renovation awakened the *joie de vivre* that had filled the house long ago.

"It had been fully restored back to its gleaming beauty," says Thom. "There aren't many rooms in the house, but they're all huge and beautiful. The ceilings are huge—twelve to thirteen feet."

As he began to work on the house and yard, his curiosity grew about who had lived there before him. Looney McCallie, a highly skilled carpenter in the north Georgia and Lookout Mountain areas, built the house in 1855 for Colonel J. J. Griffin. Thom learned that a Miss Grant—"Miss Leila," he calls her—was born there in 1891. She married Robert Wert and remained in the house until 1977. "Along that walkway that goes down were magnificent wildflowers and all kinds of things that she was very good at growing. She . . . loved fresh flowers, and at times after she'd passed away, you could smell her flowers throughout the house," says Thom. "It was either magnolia or roses. It was very strong."

Miss Leila also had a way with children. "She was so soothing that parents would drop them off, and they weren't crying anymore. They were out helping her with her plants."

A tombstone dated in the early 1900s and possibly meant for a child was found in the root cellar. But there was never evidence of a child ghost, Thom says. Miss Leila wouldn't allow such a thing. No doubt, she kept the little spirit at peace with her enchanting ways.

Thom knew right away he belonged there. He recalls feeling an "inner peace" during the years he lived in the house.

Leila Grant Wert outside the Grant House, circa 1920
Courtesy of Hilda Morse

Miss Leila seemed there still, caring for the house and those within.

"The house talks to you in a certain way. You could tell there was a presence there. . . . I don't know that anyone has ever put a finger on what it was. The feeling that I got is that it took care of the property. The spirit liked me because I was preserving the place. . . . I never saw anything bad. Instead of having the life scared out of you, it was pretty relaxing, like having life slowed down for a second. Sometimes, we called it Tranquility Island. It seemed so peaceful, almost sacred. It attracted you. People would come by all the time, and they'd just stay. The longer people stayed, the more comfortable they got. We had people spending the night. It's almost like they'd forgotten all their cares."

It seemed to Thom the house conspired to hold people in its protective shadow. "It was like breaking out of the magnetic connection there," he explains. "For some folks, it was staggering." Many visitors lost their keys or became confused when it was time to leave. One, in his bewilderment, even ran over the flowers.

The place has a long history, going back to the Cherokees' occupation of the property, Thom says. "It was harmonious for them as well."

But it wasn't so for everyone.

The house offered many a young soldier respite from the gruesome feast of blood and death during the dark autumn of 1863. The Yankees took a mighty whipping during the Battle of Chickamauga and fled toward Chattanooga. Although the house was not on the main route out of Chickamauga, thirteen miles to the south, some soldiers did pass nearby. Located near the springs just south of the Tennessee line, the home no doubt tempted many a weary soldier to stop and rest.

During November 1863, the Yankees struggled to take Lookout Mountain, five miles to the north. No battle ensued near the house, but the guns were heard there. The Union used it as a hospital. Injured men could be evacuated there easily through what is now St. Elmo. "When they were getting pinned down trying to get up the mountain, [the house was] where they were dragging them off to," says Thom. Despite the horrors of those times, Thom thinks Miss Leila turned any "bad vibrations" around.

The house or the presence within it repels negative people and attracts artistic ones. According to neighbor Hilda Morse, Miss Leila's mother, Elizabeth Grant, was musically gifted. "I'd always been told that she played for the Chicago Symphony Orchestra some," says Hilda. She even composed several pieces, including the *Kalmia Waltz*, an original printing of which remains in the Morse family as a treasured memento.

Nationally known architect Garnet Chapin later bought and worked in the house, then rented it to musicians, artists, and media types. But being the creative sort was not an automatic foot in the door. One of the most popular DJs in town moved in with Thom and his friends. He didn't have very good luck there.

"He was a bad-vibe guy, and the house did not like him," says Thom. "This radio personality was a real cocky person, really full of himself." One night, the others asked him to leave. "He was mad. He said some angry stuff. It was bad. I just no more got the thought out of my head—*That was a pretty negative thing to say*—[when] he turned away from us, lost his footing, and cracked his head. The railing, when he fell, hit him right between the eyes, split his head right open.

"There was a guy who stole something from us that was part of the house, and he had some really bad luck after that that was kinda uncanny in timing. The object that he stole, when he pawned it, got him in trouble for some other stuff. It was like it told on him."

Although Thom insists the house contains no evil, he does admit to being a bit rattled by the goings-on there. "The front right bedroom gave people a creepy feeling," he says. And the attic, known as Hell's Kitchen, seemed home to a restless entity that traveled up and down the stairway, skipping steps as it went. "There'd be a creak in a most unusual place. I heard that several times. It was like someone took a step on the first step, the center step, and the last step," skipping the rest, usually from the top down.

Like Thom, musician John Nichols was drawn to the solitary house on the hill and couldn't resist looking toward it when he drove by. "I always noticed that house—the long driveway that curved around, that big old tree at the end, the stream in the back of the house," he says. "There's a lot of energy there on that property. A lot of that area is very spiritual or even sacred."

He remembers that a famous psychic, Doc Anderson, practiced his art a few hundred feet up the road in a little red-and-white house. People came to see him from all over the world. Even Elvis was there, *before* his death in 1977.

John moved in with Thom and was soon initiated into the mystic life on the hill.

"One night," says John, "I was sitting in Thom's room in the summer, and we were just talking. The leaves were out on the trees on the side of the house, and the cars would come down [GA] 193 and cast shadows. I was looking directly out the window. All of a sudden, this car was coming, and it created this . . . perfect face of a young woman, her hair blowing in the breeze. He asked me what I had seen, and I told him. It was something I was supposed to see. The shadow was alive. It was projected there on the wall of a very well-lit room."

One night, John and Linda, another tenant, were the only people in the house. John was watching television when Linda came in. She seemed a bit edgy and demanded to talk with him. They went to a common area and sat down at a table.

"Did you go to my room last night?" she asked John.

"No. I would never come in your room ever, unless I asked you. It's none of my business."

"You're positive?"

"You know me well enough to know I'm not that kind of a person. I would never do that."

"When I woke up last night, there was someone standing over me breathing on me." The lights were out in Linda's room. She hadn't see the entity but only felt its breath.

"I'm not surprised," John said.

"What do you mean?"

John told her there were spirits in the house. "It certainly wasn't me."

One tenant, says Thom, saw an image—a man with a long beard and overalls—floating above his bed in the front right bedroom one night. He thought it resembled Looney McCallie, the carpenter who built the house.

But someone less affable than a curious carpenter lurked around the old home.

John, a truckdriver as well as a musician, came in one summer night from a routine trip hauling carpet in Dalton. It was almost dark, about eight-thirty or so, and the weather was agreeable. He pulled in under a big oak tree in the yard. "I looked in the side mirror of my car, and there was a Union soldier," he says. The soldier stood in the side yard twenty feet from the house. Short and stout, maybe in his late thirties, he had dark hair and a full beard. "I saw that as plain as day. I was stone sober. He looked like he was a ranking officer, had a couple of belts across his uniform, a pair of big boots, carrying a long saber or sword." The ghost appeared to look right at John and seemed none too friendly. "He had an ugly face on—very serious. He had a saber out, swinging it . . . back and forth."

John couldn't believe his eyes. "I looked back out my window, which was down, and there was nothing there."

Several years later, a neighbor down the road saw a soldier with a raised sword inside his home. Neither man knew about the other's experience.

After Thom, John, and the other musicians moved out, an artist moved in. Then, in 1986, Rick Williams and his wife, Kathy, now deceased, looked at the house and felt drawn to it immediately. They knew Thom and John, but news of the musicians' peculiar experiences in the house had not reached them. Not that it would've mattered. The house was just what they wanted.

Owner Garnet Chapin handed over the keys with one request. "I'm a carpenter, so he wanted me to remodel the kitchen," says Rick.

When Rick began the kitchen renovation that summer, he discovered some of his tools missing. He assumed Kathy, the only other person there, had borrowed them.

"Honey, did you get my saw, my hammer?" he asked.

"Rick, I haven't touched your saw."

Twice the tools disappeared, then reappeared in the backyard near a lady's horse-mounting block.

"I knew I didn't do it," says Rick. "I protect my tools. My dad was a house builder, and he taught me how to take care of tools."

Rick didn't know an apparition fitting the description of Looney McCallie had been seen by a former resident, so he had no idea who would take such an interest in his tools. He just felt grateful they hadn't been damaged or stolen.

"I also had a band at the time, the Sherman Williams Band, and we'd have rehearsals there. We'd be in rehearsals in the afternoon, and the lights would come on and go off. It's an old house—I passed that off completely. We'd come home from playing, and the lights would be flickering off and on. We had turned all the lights off when we left, except for the back-porch light. The TV would go off when we were watching a football game or something. I told Garnet, 'You need to check the wiring on this.' And he'd tell me it'd been rewired."

Soon, the Williamses were introduced to the enchanting hostess who had so bewitched the earlier tenants. But not face to face. The feminine presence manifested herself through her affection for babies and animals.

"I remember it like it was yesterday," says Rick. "We had a pet rabbit that was supposed to be a dwarf, and it turned out to be about sixteen pounds. It was a horse. So we had to keep her in a cage in the upstairs hallway."

On Saturday mornings, Rick explains, it was Kathy's habit to lift Emma out of the cage, bring her to the bed, and let her hop around. One morning, Kathy had gone down the hall to retrieve Emma. Suddenly, she let out a cry of surprise, startling Rick.

"What's wrong?" he asked.

"Smell this rabbit!" Kathy brought Emma into the bedroom and held her under Rick's nose.

"She smelled like the strongest rose perfume," he says. "It was all over the rabbit's hair. It was so strong it was pungent. It just knocked me down. Nobody's got perfume like that. I said, 'I can't stand this.' It was overwhelming."

Nobody was home but the two of them. Rick asked Kathy what she had done to the rabbit. Kathy denied she had done anything. For her part, Emma seemed unconcerned.

"We couldn't explain it," says Rick. "That's when Kathy

said, 'I think this place has a ghost, I really do.' "

One night, friends Scott and Deb and their little daughter Ashley—about nine months old—came for dinner. It was their first visit to the house. Scott went upstairs to the bathroom, carrying the baby. Suddenly, Ashley started cooing, as if someone were playing or talking with her. "She was going, 'Oooh, oooh,' " says Rick. "Scott said he had this warm feeling come over him."

While Scott was upstairs, Kathy told Deb about the perfumed rabbit. Scott heard nothing about it.

Later, as they drove home through St. Elmo, Deb relayed the story about Emma to Scott. "He ran off the road," Rick says.

Afterward, Scott told Deb, "I knew it. I just felt like somebody was up there."

That somebody watched over the basement as well.

The Williamses took in a stray German shepherd mix they named Trooper.

"One night, it was extremely cold, so we closed off one of the very small rooms downstairs, put Trooper in, and locked the door with a hook latch," Rick says.

The next morning when Kathy scooped Emma up and brought her into the bedroom, Trooper ambled in behind them.

Rick was surprised. "How did you get out?" he asked Trooper.

Trooper wouldn't say.

"Kathy, did you let Trooper out?"

"Rick, I haven't even been downstairs."

Rick went down and found the latch undone. He couldn't think of any way the dog might have unlatched the hook from the inside, and there was no other way out.

Trooper enjoyed life at the house in the country. He welcomed the humans who dropped in—with one exception. "If one of my friends came up with dark hair and a dark beard, he would eat him up," says Rick. "He attacked one friend and tore his Levi's."

Rick felt sure Trooper's last owner must have been a man with dark hair and a beard who had abused him. He knew nothing of the scowling and bearded Yankee soldier John Nichols had seen waving a saber in the side yard. Trooper may have known the soldier well.

Miss Leila could have known that Yankee soldier, too. Unknown to John and Rick, Miss Leila's father was Hemen W. Grant, captain of the Fourth Michigan Volunteer Cavalry at Chickamauga and Chattanooga. His regiment was actively engaged in the battles and scouting missions around north Georgia. Perhaps he saw the white house while out on sorties with his men and, like so many after him, was beckoned to return.

The house continues to reach out across the years to those it seeks. Hundreds of children visit each year to meander through Rock City's adjoining Enchanted Maize and romp on the playground in the front field. Miss Leila still knows how to beguile the little ones entrusted to her warm and fragrant arms. As for those who do not appreciate her Southern hospitality, one gruff Yankee stands ready to send them on their way.

green eyes searching in the night

CHICKAMAUGA, GEORGIA

Battlefields are surely the most haunted of places. Death can come instantly, leaving the soul shocked and confused. Or slowly and agonizingly, imprinting the horror of violent destruction on the spirit and overcoming, at least temporarily, its instinct to pass on to its proper realm. Dying and frightened comrades also lost in the gray void surround the confused soul, holding it back and being held back in turn. With so many reliving their last moments over and over and over, the battle never ends. Such a place is Chickamauga.

Some say the Battle of Chickamauga still rages. After the tourists leave for the day, the souls of long-dead soldiers rise up to roam the field in search of fallen comrades, the enemy, or perhaps their own lost corpses.

The battle, which burst onto the quiet countryside September 19 and 20, 1863, was one of the bloodiest of a

Snodgrass Hill, favorite stalking ground for Green Eyes, is considered by many to be the most haunted place in the Chattanooga area.

bloody war. That corner of north Georgia was no great prize. But nearby Chattanooga was, and Union major general William S. Rosecrans wanted it. His Army of the Cumberland marched out of Murfreesboro, Tennessee, intent on capturing Chattanooga's railroads, lifeline of the Confederacy in the Western theater. Rosecrans's movements forced Confederate general Braxton Bragg and his Army of Tennessee to fall back from Middle Tennessee to Chattanooga on the Georgia-Tennessee line. When Rosecrans's army came down through the rugged ridges of northeastern Alabama and northwestern Georgia in an attempt to cut Bragg's railroad supply line, Bragg abandoned Chattanooga and moved south to LaFayette, Georgia. With more than a hundred thousand blue and gray troops moving through the area, the little farming community nestled in the valley of West Chickamauga Creek was fated to witness one of the most horrible scenes of death and anguish ever on American soil.

The men destiny had placed in this most awful place seemed doomed from the start. Even the weather conspired against them. During the six weeks before the battle, there had been almost no rain. The day before the fighting, the temperature was mild, in the mid-sixties. But that evening, the half-moon set around midnight, leaving the sky gloomy and forbidding. Then the temperature dropped thirty degrees the night of September 19, and an unseasonable frost occurred the morning of September 20, followed by a heavy fog, especially near Chickamauga Creek.

Describing the night between the two days of battle, Confederate general John B. Gordon wrote, "The feint [sic] moonlight, almost wholly shut out by dense foliage, added to the weird spell of the sombre scene. In every direction were dimly burning tapers, carried by nurses and relief corps searching for the wounded. All over the field lay the unburied dead, their pale faces made ghastlier by streaks of blood and clotted hair, and black stains of powder left upon their lips when they tore off with their teeth the ends of deadly cartridges. At nine o'clock on that Sabbath morning, September 20, as the church bells of Chattanooga summoned its children to Sunday school, the signal-guns sounding through the forests of Chickamauga called the bleeding armies again to battle."

The fog, fortified by the smoke of battle, evaporated by midmorning on September 20, revealing ruin on a grand scale. Surveying the gory scene, one Confederate general described Chickamauga Creek as a "river of death." Bloody Pond earned its gruesome name when the blood of dead and dying soldiers and horses who had crawled there to quench their thirst emptied into the once-clear water. Estimates vary, but it appears nearly four thousand men were killed and over twenty-six thousand wounded. Another nineteen hundred went missing, most of them likely dead. Some soldiers may have suffered moderate wounds and died of shock during the unseasonably cold nights, especially if they were without blankets. Some wounded were agonizingly burned to death when they were overtaken by forest fires consuming the dry, tangled forests. Others crept off to hide and die. The dead and dying littered McFarland Road into Rossville. Confusion ruled the day.

It is unknown how many ghosts haunt the rolling fields of Chickamauga. Park visitors tell stories of weird encounters with the inexplicable. Eerie sights and the sounds of phantom gunshots, footsteps, hoofbeats, and groans are common on this bloody ground.

The most famous of Chickamauga's unquiet spirits is Green Eyes. Those unfortunate enough to find themselves within park boundaries after sunset may well see his disembodied, glowing eyes patrolling the dark battlefield. The reason behind his ceaseless mission remains a mystery. According to some locals, Green Eyes was a Confederate officer who led a small group of horsemen on the battlefield. Almost all of them were killed. Today, their commanding officer can be seen tearing across the field at full gallop. Witnesses have sighted him on bridges. Some claim he bolts down the hill from Wilder Tower. His horse has been observed crying.

The impetuous general Nathan Bedford Forrest might have inspired the tale of the fabled riders. He and seventy of his Tennessee horsemen sparked a skirmish when they unexpectedly encountered Union soldiers. Several lives were lost in the initial confrontation, including a prominent doctor whose head was blown from his body.

One of Forrest's cavalry officers wrote, "Neighing horses, wild and frightened, were running in every direction; whistling, seething, crackling bullets, the piercing, screaming fragments of shells, the whirring sound of shrapnel and the savage shower of canister, mingled with the fierce answering yells of defiance, all united in one horrible sound."

He had never seen a battle so awful. "The ghastly, mangled dead and horribly wounded strewed the earth for over half a mile up and down the river banks," he wrote. "The dead were piled upon each other in ricks, like cordwood, to make passage for advancing columns." Chickamauga Creek "ran red with blood."

Others believe the Green Eyes legend might derive from a historical report lauding heroic Union colonel John Wilder and his brigade of mounted infantrymen from Indiana and Illinois. They tried valiantly to hold an area south of Snodgrass Hill against General James Longstreet's onslaught but failed.

The white limestone tower erected in 1902 to honor Wilder and his men has been the site of several suicides and other peculiar goings-on. Over the years, there have been at least a couple of accidents nearby involving drivers who believed they saw Green Eyes. "They got all psyched up and ran off the road at high speed," says former ranger Bob Keebler.

The *Catoosa County News* reported that some teenagers out on a hayride near Wilder Tower in 1990 spotted a flaming torch and heard the sound of hooves. As the ghostly green-eyed horse drew near, the group beheld its rider—a skeleton on which a Confederate uniform hung. The gruesome form seemed to dismount, muttering "Amy, Amy" again and again before finally disappearing.

Or was he perhaps saying "enemy"?

Another tale, says Patrice Hobbs Glass, who grew up in nearby LaFayette, centers on the Wisconsin Cavalry Monument, also known as "the Riderless Horse," which is near Wilder Tower to the west, across Chickamauga-Vittetoe Road. A widow of an officer killed during the battle treasured a pair of emerald earrings he had given her before he was called away forever. In tribute to him, she donated the emeralds to be mounted as eyes in this statue commemorating the bravery and sacrifice of his fallen men. The emeralds were in place the evening before the unveiling service. The next morning as the crowd watched, officials ceremoniously uncovered the statue. The precious stones had vanished. The officer had reclaimed his wife's earrings and set out to find her. The emeralds blaze brightly as he wanders the battlefield longing for her, his soul mate.

One Green Eyes legend centers on the Rider-less Horse, erected to commemorate the deeds of the First Wisconsin Cavalry.

Seventeen-year-old Denise Nelson encountered a set of mysterious green eyes in 1980. Having taken the shortcut home to Chickamauga after her shift at the Krystal restaurant in Fort Oglethorpe, Denise was driving through the S curve not far from Wilder Tower at about three o'clock in the morning. She crept through the mist rising off the wet road edged in a shroud of tall, dripping trees. Amid this dark landscape, a darker shape appeared. Denise was startled by its "brilliant green" eyes, level with her own and only twenty feet away. The creature quickly faded into the forest. "I sped up to get the heck out of there," she says.

Denise has lived in the area her entire life and seen many wild animals. But she insists it wasn't a raccoon, a squirrel, or even a deer. Maybe it was a bear or panther, she began to think as the years went by. Regardless, she stopped using that route. "I just went down the main drag after that," she says.

Perhaps what Denise saw *was* a big cat, just not a panther. Some people believe Green Eyes roams the park in the form of a tiger. This legend is inspired by the monument on Snodgrass Hill memorializing Opdyke's Tiger Regiment, the 125th Ohio Volunteers. This unit of nearly a thousand men was caught in the rout but managed to regroup on the hill, where Longstreet

Many believe Green Eyes prowls in the form of a tiger atop the monument to Opdyke's 125th Ohio.

assaulted it. Seventeen men died, eighty-three were wounded, and five were never found. It is said the grieving tiger leaves his stone at night and prowls the park, seeking out his men lost in battle. His eyes glow green in the murky shadows, especially when they fall on intruders.

Others whisper of an appalling possibility—Green Eyes is more ancient than the soldiers in blue or gray. The battlefield was once a hunting ground for the Cherokees and likely an earlier, nameless tribe that mysteriously disappeared, leaving behind a few artifacts and one indigenous demon. Some say Green Eyes was seen *during* the battle, creeping among the dead and near dead. Was this ghoulish entity present long before the white man's madness, part of a dark past lost to history? Or was it lured to the battlefield by the unspeakable horror of new death and despair?

Chattanooga Valley resident Mike Moore believes Green Eyes is a demon. "My friends tell me that when Green Eyes is in the battlefield, the ghosts leave—because he's not a ghost. He is a demon from hell. He smells like sulfur, and it's ice cold in his trail."

Do ghosts fear demons?

"I'd have to say yes," says Mike. "They don't like 'em."

Contemporary folks claim to have seen a longhaired, fanged apparition walking upright beneath a flapping cape. Former chief ranger Ed Tinney told *Catoosa County News* reporter Kevin Cummings that in 1976, he was walking along Glenn-Kelly Road at about four in the morning. "He encountered a man over 6 feet tall, wearing a long black duster, with shaggy, stringy black waist-length hair, walking toward him," wrote Cummings. Afraid of being attacked, Tinney crossed the road. "When the man became parallel with Tinney, he turned and smiled a devilish grin, and his dark eyes glistened." Fortunately, a car approached. When the headlights hit the menacing figure, it vanished.

John Hodges spent hours as a teenager cruising the park with classmates, hoping to see Green Eyes. Shortly after midnight one cold fall evening in 1964, Hodges, his brother Jim, and four East Ridge High School seniors were riding in a Ford convertible near Wilder Tower. They left the car and walked twenty to thirty yards into a field. Seemingly out of nowhere, a light appeared. The boys didn't think much of it. It was probably a car, they figured. The light, which Hodges estimates was five to six feet off the ground, turned bluish green, came closer and closer through the trees and brush, then split in two about a hundred yards away. The boys could not even draw breath to scream. They sprinted to the car and dove in, not bothering to open the doors. As the car tore away, a loud noise like a gunshot assaulted them. All ducked while shrieking, "Let's go!"

Later, they discovered a rod under the car had cracked. The mechanic told them that only extreme heat could cause such damage. They could not fathom how the rod could have reached such a temperature on a night so chilly. The boys never went back to the battlefield after dark. Jim Hodges, who played tackle for the Memphis State football team, spoke for all the boys: "It scared the pee out of me."

Lakeview-Fort Oglethorpe High School student Blake Burnette grew up in the park. Though he doesn't accept most of what he hears about Green Eyes, he does believe Green Eyes exists. He has seen the glowing eyes. "I didn't have a light, so it couldn't have been a 'possum," he says.

One evening while camping in the park with Boy Scout Troop 8, he spotted a large creature. He and a couple of other scouts were wrestling in the field across from and slightly south of the Florida Monument on LaFayette Road. It was dark but clear, a quarter-moon in the sky.

During the melee, Blake happened to glance toward the highway several hundred feet away. "I saw something really big cross the road in the headlights," he says. "I guess it was seven and a half to eight feet tall. It wasn't wearing any clothes. It was hairy. It started walking across the road, but then it went into a little gallop on all fours. The car was coming, and it didn't want to be caught or hit."

Blake hollered for the other boys to look, but too late. The creature was gone.

"It was either a grizzly bear or Green Eyes, and I'm pretty sure there's no grizzly bears in the park," Blake says.

His friend Drew Jennings, also of Troop 8, did not see the creature but believes Blake. "I've known him since middle school. I'd trust anything he'd say. He's an Eagle Scout."

Blake thinks the creature is the spirit of "a Civil War soldier that got betrayed or got messed over" and is bent on revenge. Back when Fort Oglethorpe was an active army post, Blake has heard, Green Eyes would kill people. "Even before that, in the 1870s, he would kill old Union soldiers. Or people would just disappear." Others, he says, would be found "mauled, not by a coyote but something bigger." Still, Blake will not say the entity is evil. "You don't mess with him, and he don't mess with you."

Blake admits, "I do believe in ghosts." He and Drew will continue to camp in the park with Troop 8, eyes and ears open.

Eleven members of the Snodgrass family once enjoyed a peaceful life in this small cabin.

fifes and drums

CHICKAMAUGA, GEORGIA

Parents often tell their children that they make so much noise, they could wake the dead. One group of rowdy boys discovered that indeed they could.

Having grown up as one of six children, Scoutmaster Doug Albritton knows the best way to keep kids in line is to run them ragged. So one sticky summer evening around ten-thirty, he took about ten wound-up boys—his Cub Scout Pack 3140 and some older campers from Troop 8—to play capture the flag on Snodgrass Hill, the site of fierce fighting during the 1863 Battle of Chickamauga.

The Scouts planted the flags, left one lantern at the bottom of the hill, and set another at the top, closer to the Snodgrass Cabin. The chasing and screaming started as soon as the boys were set free on the sacred grass. Scouts Blake

Burnette and Bryan Russell and a small group of Cub Scouts held the high ground while Doug, Scout Ben Bouvier, and the other younger boys defended the flags.

Not long into the scrimmage, the boys at the top began hearing music that sounded like flutes and drums.

"We thought people were trying to mess with us," says Blake.

An hour passed, and the strains of battle music played on. Feeling responsible for the younger boys, the teenagers thought it best to tell an adult. If pranksters were in the park, Doug needed to know. "One of the older Scouts, Blake, came rushing down," says Doug.

"We heard drums in the woods," he told Doug. "I want you to come and investigate."

"When I was a Scout," says Doug, "we loved to play jokes on younger Scouts to try to scare the bejeebies out of them. So I thought they were playing a joke on me." He thought, *Well, I'll play along and go up and see what's going on.*

Midnight was closing in on them. Doug sent the Cub Scouts back to camp and started up toward the cabin with some of the older boys. He heard the drums. "It sounded like a snare drum." As he crept closer, he heard fife music. "It sounded like Civil War-type music. It made me feel just a little bit weird." His mind raced. What could it be? Visitors listening to CDs? He knew there was no electricity near the hill. One car—empty, as far as he could tell—was parked nearby.

He couldn't help imagining what had happened there in 1863 to the soldiers struggling for possession of the hill and to the Snodgrass family, who barely escaped the battle alive. George Snodgrass and his third wife, Elizabeth, built the homestead around 1851 on 160 rolling acres of meadow, pasture, and forest. The property included a log cabin, sheds, and a garden with an oak-rail fence as protection from roaming livestock. However, the fence was little protection against unwanted guests when an army large in number but short on supplies prowled the area looking for food. The family encountered their first Yankees as waves of starving men pillaged the countryside, grabbing sweet potatoes, livestock, and anything else a human could eat. Worse was to come.

At about two o'clock in the afternoon on September 19, the din of battle literally hit home. Bullets began falling on the roof. Mr. Snodgrass ordered his family of ten—minus one son on the field in the Confederates ranks—to flee northwest with neighbors to the safety of a wooded ravine. The Federals took Snodgrass Hill and, under heavy fire, held it with the obstinacy of a mule in a briar patch. They commandeered the little cabin and transformed it into a primitive field hospital. On September 20, the tide of battle turned. General George Thomas's Yankees retreated north to Chattanooga. General James Longstreet's victorious Rebels captured the hill and the house, filling it with their own wounded.

The refugees in the ravine listened to the cracking, roaring storm of battle, waiting and praying for deliverance. This account by Julia Kittie Snodgrass, only six years old at the time of the battle, was reported in a 1923 *Chattanooga News* article: "Late on Sunday afternoon, as the firing gradually died down on Snodgrass hill, the party *suddenly heard a band strike up some southern air* [italics added]. They divined that this meant victory for the Confederates, and as their sympathies were with that side, jubilation broke out among them. Some of the women sang and shouted aloud in the excess of their joy."

The cheers gave way to anguish. Long after the battle, injured men lay struggling for life inside the Snodgrass Cabin. The family was not allowed back for eight days and nights. When they did return, they found the once-cozy home a grisly shambles of broken furniture and bloody gore. The family fled once more, not to return until the end of the war. Julia Kittie Snodgrass, reported the *Chattanooga News*, recalled riding away from her home south toward Ringgold, Georgia, assailed by the most horrible sights and smells—"splintered and broken timber, arms and accoutrements scattered about, bloody and shell shattered breastworks, dead men and dead horses, yet unburied."

As Doug passed the monuments and cannons leading to the log house, visions of the tangled carnage that had once covered the quiet pastures and woods assaulted him. The Angel of Death had swooped down 140 years before and snatched legions of souls atop the very hill on which he and the boys were walking.

Doug and the Scouts tightened their ranks and eased forward. "As we got closer to the cabin, the music stopped. It started raining." Doug was about to suggest they pack it up and hoof it back to camp when they heard footsteps scatter away from them into the woods.

He points to the upward-sloping area south of the cabin. "It was maybe a dozen people." He insists it wasn't deer. "It sounded like the two-footed kind of animal. I thought that was really odd, another reason I didn't want to approach the cabin. I told the boys that for whatever reason, we're probably not supposed to be up here." It was almost Sunday, and Doug felt uneasy about being in the presence of unknown entities so close to the Sabbath. They headed back.

Doug later asked a park ranger if he'd ever heard or seen anything on the battlefield. "He denied it." But then, says Doug, up until that time, he'd never encountered anything either, though he was a frequent park visitor.

"I don't know if I'm a believer in ghosts or not, but I know what I heard," he says. "It sure makes a good story for little boys when they sit around the campfire now."

Cub Scout Pack 3140 continues to camp in the park. Huddled around a slow blaze, the boys still whisper tales of Snodgrass Hill.

dark, dark road

CHICKAMAUGA, GEORGIA

Farmers are rugged and self-reliant individualists who face all manner of threats and hardships without complaint. But even the toughest of men can be spooked when sunlight bleeds away from the battlefield of Chickamauga. One local farmer admits that, when night cloaks these haunted north Georgia fields, he is scared of the dark.

Jimmy Haun is not a ranger or historian. Nonetheless, this farmer earns part of his living on the Chickamauga battlefield. The last few years, he has contracted to cut hay on park property, a job that requires him to stay in the fields until the job is done or night falls, whichever comes first.

Though Jimmy doesn't put much credence in ghosts, he won't be caught in the park after dark. "Go out at midnight and stand around for about fifteen minutes," he says. "You'll leave with a respect for the place, I promise you that."

Jimmy didn't feel any foreboding about jogging in the park two or three times a week or working there long hours in the summer mowing and hauling hay. Still, things were not quite normal. More than once in midsummer, he saw a Confederate soldier standing in the tall grass next to a cannon at the top of the hill in the thirteen-acre parcel across from Lytle Field and west of the Dyer House. The hefty soldier wore sturdy, tall boots and had pulled his pointed gray felt hat down over his eyes, shading his face from Jimmy. Like many visitors to the park, the soldier, his arm propped on a cannon wheel, watched Jimmy as he passed back and forth on his tractor. "I drove right by him. But he never acknowledged me. I waved at him, and he never waved back. He just stood there."

This struck Jimmy as odd. He wondered if the man had something on his mind. It just wasn't right—a person not waving. Although the whole scene perplexed him, Jimmy was not ready to concede the man was anything but flesh and blood, probably a rogue reenactor. "I wouldn't know a ghost if I saw it."

Jimmy will go to the park anytime, as long as it's not dark. "It's a different place at night. It's just a different feeling altogether. I used to haul hay all night, especially in the summer. It's a lot cooler. If it's gonna rain, I'd haul all that hay in. I didn't wanna lose it. I'd spent all that time getting it baled. I didn't want it wet."

Jimmy Haun sometimes sees a brooding Confederate soldier standing near this cannon commemorating Dent's Alabama Battery.

Jimmy would enter the park by Chickamauga-Vittetoe Road close to where the horses unload north of Wilder Tower, then drive north past Lytle Field. "It's dark out there at night. I mean it's really dark, especially if it's cloudy."

Jimmy used an old dump truck that could haul eighty bales at a time. So he might make ten trips in a single evening if he had cut a field yielding eight hundred bales. Then he'd have to go back one more time to get his tractor. He sometimes saw or heard things at two-thirty or three in the morning that he wasn't too sure about—strange flashing white lights and the sounds of birds of prey, maybe. But he still wasn't worried.

"It got to where my lights wouldn't come on in the park. They'd just go off right there in front of Lytle Field going out [Chickamauga-Vittetoe Road]. I carry a load about every hour and a half. And it does it every time. You're driving thirty or thirty-five miles an hour, and they go off. You don't have the time you think you have. You just stop. You can't see! It is dark in the park at night. I've leaned out and [crept] just to see. And once I got outside the park, they'd come back on."

Jimmy, like most farmers, is mechanically inclined. He'd get out his tools to fix the lights. "I changed everything on them things. I'm not perfect. It could be a weird short, but it'd really be weird."

He says the roads are rough as a cob in the park, but then so are the roads on his farm, and they don't cause the lights to go out. "I've driven it everywhere. The only place it does it is that park. It's the *only* place it ever happens. I've never figured it out."

He also began to worry he'd have no one to come get him if he wrecked in the dark. "My wife won't go in there at night by herself. She don't feel safe in there at night. If I broke down, I don't know what I'd do."

So he decided to quit working hay at night in the park. "The lights [going out] were the straw that broke the camel's back. I just felt I'd hurt myself. So I don't haul hay at night anymore. I don't really believe in spirits, but I believe that some things are just better left alone."

ALABAMA ON HIS MIND?

Who is the Confederate soldier? Jimmy, who admits he's no Civil War buff, has no clue who fought atop the knoll in 1863 or what the outcome was. A quick look at the historical marker between the two cannons reveals the story. As in most areas of the park, several waves of soldiers struggled for possession of the unnamed hill. But the two big guns now tucked into the edge of the hayfield commemorate the cannoneers who made it their own—Dent's Alabama Battery. At noon on September 20, Captain Dent's men, on hearing ferocious firing to the northwest, moved into position to inflict further pain on Federal troops retreating through the mouth of McFarland Gap. The Alabama boys' quick thinking resulted in a blocked road and allowed their comrades to capture many wagons and caissons.

Still, if the Confederate soldier Jimmy saw is one of the victors, the story behind his brooding posture will likely remain a mystery.

dead boys walking

FORT OGLETHORPE, GEORGIA

Young men fight our wars because they believe death will not claim them. Three teenagers maintained that sad illusion for 145 years until they met a man from another century who pointed the way home.

It was a clear night on Park City Road north of the Chickamauga battlefield. Mike Moore was visiting his friend Karen at her mobile home at the foot of the wooded ridge south of GA 2A in Fort Oglethorpe.

Karen had told Mike that during the anniversary of the battle fought September 19 and 20, 1863, you could hear the clanging and hoofbeats of men riding horses across the hill just north of McFarland Gap. At other times of the year, a phantom woman in early-twentieth-century dress would walk down from an old homeplace on the ridge and into Karen's yard.

Mike was curious about the supernormal occurrences, but that evening was *not* the likely time to hear the phantom horsemen. Nor was the ghostly woman walking. It was late summer in 1999, and all seemed quiet. At two o'clock that morning, Mike and Karen ventured outside to enjoy the evening. The luminous moon was making its way across a silent sky above the sounds of crickets and occasional traffic in the distance. It was so still they heard the gentle thumps of early acorns hitting the ground.

That's when the spirits came. A small white sphere appeared in the thick grove of oaks nearby. Unlike the steely moon beyond, it glowed pale and translucent. Karen turned to Mike, stunned. "There's your ghost!"

"It was like a basketball sitting in the top of an oak tree, but it was white like an orb," says Mike. "It looked like it was rolling around the limbs. It would land on a limb, and once it came off the limbs, it started falling like a waterfall. And about halfway down the waterfall, it started turning into two more waterfalls."

When the waterfalls reached the ground, three human-sized figures appeared and stood within a few feet of Mike, who had moved toward them as they took shape. Keeping a safe distance, Karen saw the apparitions, too, but only as three formless white mists.

A powerful psychic energy rushed toward Mike from the three entities.

"I felt—and I don't know if this was real—that they were three young men in Union uniforms. These guys were already dead, and they were heading toward Chattanooga. They were kids, just little boys," he says.

Mike pauses, visibly distraught as he recalls the sad sight. "One was a poor little nineteen-year-old with a bullet hole in him that big." He presses his hands, stretched in a circle six inches wide, against his stomach. "The others were carrying him, and they weren't in much better shape. They were dead, but two of them were *staring* at me."

Mike describes the figures as white, but not ghostly white. "They were white because they'd lost so much blood. They'd lost all their blood running up through there. They were in shock. The strongest one of them, who had his arm around the weakest, he never did look at me. He kept looking back, so I knew the Rebels were in pursuit. He never did pay any attention. The other two had that open look."

Did the spirits see him?

"Yes," he says firmly. One in particular seemed dumbfounded. "He may have felt like he was seeing a ghost by seeing me. He was soon to die. They were lost. They were so lost."

Mike isn't sure what they thought of the encounter, but he feels the soldiers wanted an answer from him. They had to learn the truth of their deaths. "I had to tell them."

He said aloud, "You're dead. It's time for you to go."

"I told them that they died a hundred years ago, that they were mortally wounded at the Battle of Chickamauga. I told them, 'Follow the light.' After I told them to go to the light, it vaporized back into the ball. As it was clearing the trees, it was gone."

Since that night, Karen has moved away, and Mike has not returned there. He heard two years later that a neighbor committed suicide within twenty feet of where the apparitions formed. But he believes and hopes that the three lost souls he saw that summer night went on to find their peace.

The never-ending clash of battle continues for untold numbers of less fortunate soldiers lost in the forests and fields around Chickamauga. The roads, byways, and rough trails leading out of the area witnessed—and maybe still do—the passage of routed Yankee regiments desperate to reach Chattanooga.

"All along the road, for miles, wounded men were lying," wrote Union general John Beatty of the retreat through nearby McFarland Gap. "They had crawled or hobbled slowly away from the fury of the battle, become exhausted, and lay down by the roadside to die."

When they found the main avenues of retreat—such as McFarland Gap—clogged with their fellows or held by the enemy, they broke and fled like ants from a fire, each man for himself, over the rolling ridges and through ditches and wild tangles, in a desperate dash for safety. Some never made it out.

How many are there yet?

Maybe too many. "There are still tales that you can hear the horses and the cavalry coming across that hill," says Mike.

But three blue boys on foot have found their way home at last.

Reluctant Seer

Mike Moore is the picture of rural north Georgia manhood—a good ol' Southern Baptist boy, cattleman, and former railroad hand with a knack for transforming rusty wrecks into classic cars. At home behind the wheel of a four-wheel-drive pickup, shotgun in tow, he wrestled for years with the incongruity of an inherited—and unwelcome—ability to sense ghosts. Believing in ghosts, not to mention having contact with them, was at odds with all he understood and held dear about himself and God's creation. Now, he accepts it, although he feels his understanding of the phenomenon is limited at best. "I'm just a first-grader," he says.

miss clarissa's angry yankee

CHICKAMAUGA, GEORGIA

Brutal, violent death imprints many a soldier's soul. But wounded pride can cut just as deeply. A ghost so hurt, like a spiteful child, can nurse a grudge for decades, lashing out against his perceived tormentors when they, unknowing, cross into his shadowy domain. Where such a ghost prowls, sometimes a gentle soul remains, too, to watch over the living and tarry awhile within familiar walls.

Some might say Betts Jewell was born clutching a clod of red Georgia clay, so attuned is she to the land of her ancestors. She speaks in the warm Southern lilt that is fast fading even in the countryside, and the subjects she speaks of most often are family, church, farming, and the past.

For Betts, the past can be the present, since she lives in a haunted house.

She knew the history of the old home when she and her new husband, Charlie Berry, moved into the sturdy Chickamauga house in 1978. James Hunt built it in the 1830s after the Cherokee land lottery, she says. He married Betts's

The portrait of Miss Clarissa hangs in the old homeplace still, keeping watch over the Berry family.
Courtesy of Hunt family history

great-uncle's grandmother, Clarissa Gordon, then left her widowed at a young age before the Civil War. She was a plucky, strong-willed woman who kept the farm going and the family—two girls and two boys—together.

When the Berrys settled in, the home had changed little from Miss Clarissa's day, with the exception of a few minor modifications made during the mid-twentieth century. Some of the furniture is original to the house, and Miss Clarissa's portrait still presides over the living room. Maybe Miss Clarissa herself remains as matron of the old homestead, for it seems an unseen someone shares the rooms and hallways with Charlie, Betts, and their two boys.

"When Charlie and I first got married, he heard people walking around in the house all the time at night. He would get up with his service revolver—he had been an Atlanta policeman for twelve years," Betts says. "Sometimes at night, I'll wake up in a start because I've heard someone talking or heard a noise. Who knows if I've just dreamed it or really heard it?"

The house suffered through some frightful moments during the 1863 Battle of Chickamauga. Cannonballs tore through the wall, and minié balls pelted the house like hail in a fierce wind. Troops scoured the countryside, pillaging farmsteads for food and supplies.

"There are several stories that have been told and passed down, and we're not sure if they're true or not," Betts says. "When soldiers came through the house, one soldier, a young man, had headed up the attic stairs to check and see what was hidden in the attic. Miss Clarissa told him not to go up there, that that was none of his business. But he continued up the stairs, and she either pulled on his coattails or she pushed him. The soldier fell backwards and broke his shoulder. He was so angry he drew his pistol to shoot her. His commanding officer, who had witnessed the whole thing, told him if he was going to let a woman push him around, he certainly wasn't going to allow him to kill her. So her life was spared."

But the young soldier's pride was not. He left the house in shame. Or did he? Some of the strange goings-on there make visitors wonder if he has returned to seek his revenge—all the more so because the story of his comeuppance has been passed down, written up, and retold around Chickamauga for the amusement of the ladies for years.

Yes, he might have enjoyed a moment of glee when he heard that, after the incident, Union men took Miss Clarissa away to Crawfish Springs—now Chickamauga—for questioning. She'd sassed the Yankees one time too many. Previously, according to historian E. Raymond Evans, she had sat down on a shot hog and refused to let a pillaging soldier take it. "It'll rot before *you* get it!" she said. Then another soldier shot her wash pot. "She told him that it was a brave soldier that would burst a widow's wash pot," writes Evans.

But the soldier's pleasure at her interrogation was short-lived. "They kept her for several days, then allowed her to come back home unharmed," Betts says. Worse days were to come.

Betts believes that Clarissa and her four children, in their late teens and early twenties, were still home when the Battle of Chickamauga began. During the heat of the action, Miss Clarissa and her children left and went to her parents' house, the Gordon home. They stayed there until the worst of the battle was over. "She, her mother, and a slave went back to check and see if the house was still standing," Betts says. "When they got there, there were two dead Yankee soldiers on the front porch. They were afraid that they'd be accused of killing the soldiers. So the two women and the slave pulled the soldiers down the hill—we don't know which hill because the house sits on a little knoll—and buried them."

Evans writes that at least two Confederate soldiers were buried on the Hunt farm. "We had taken one young man out of Mrs. Hunt's cellar," wrote neighbor W. H. Henderson, quoted by Evans. "He was shot in the head[. L]etters in his pockets [indicated] he was from South Carolina. We carried him to the top of the hill north of Mrs. Hunt's on the right side of the road where another was killed. We buried both of the boys in one grave."

All four soldiers lie on the farm still.

The peculiar incidents escalated when Betts and Charlie began updating the old home. One bathroom had already been added in the 1940s or late 1930s. "When we moved in, we redid rooms, but we didn't do any major construction," Betts says. "We took one of the small bedrooms and made it

Clarissa Hunt's house at the end of the nineteenth century.
Courtesy of Hunt family history

into a bathroom." They also gutted the kitchen. Minié balls rained down on them. As is often the case with house renovation, the spirits within were agitated.

Strange problems continue to plague the new construction.

"The lights go off and on at will," Betts says. "I had the electrical problem checked. I had trouble with that one wall before we expanded the house. I had James [an electrician] come out and check it to see if there was a short in the electrical circuits. There was not. Then we knocked down that wall, and I thought we wouldn't have any more problems with it. I'll be John Brown if we still don't have problems, and the light still just comes on. Most of the time, they'll be on and just go off. The switch will be on. If you flip the switch, it doesn't do anything.

"Also in the same corner where that wall is, in the kitchen, three different workers fell off the ladder, including me. I just fell over backwards for no reason at all. I think I was wallpapering. It was the strangest thing. I just fell over backwards. Johnny Boles [the contractor] hurt his back when he fell." Betts shakes her head, still baffled by the accident. She says all three victims were experienced with ladders.

When the work was finished, whatever or whoever had been disturbed by the construction continued to harass the Berrys. "After we added on the bedroom and bathroom and expanded the kitchen, you could turn on the tub faucet, and the sink faucet would just start running. Sometimes when the washing machine was going, the bathroom sink would come on. And sometimes when you would flush the toilet in the other part of the house, the sink would start running. That sink is on the same wall as the one that gives us trouble in the kitchen.

"After we finished the construction on the house, we had a Fourth of July party. Friends came over, and we were talking about the water. They didn't believe me, so we all had to come into the bathroom. We had two or three couples in there. I turned on the tub faucet, and the water in the sink came on. The handle never turned, it just came on. So then I turned it off, and the sink faucet went off."

Betts's friend Joni asked if she could try. She turned the handle, but the sink faucet didn't come on. Then she turned it off. "This is spooky," she said.

Scott, another friend, asked Betts to turn it again. "So I did it again, and the water came on again," Betts says.

Tammy, Scott's wife, turned the tub faucet on, and the sink faucet didn't come on. They thought Betts was pulling a trick by turning the tub faucet a certain way. They asked Betts to turn it on one more time so they could watch exactly what she was doing. "So I turned it on," says Betts. "And all I did was just turn the faucet, and it came on."

"This is it. We're leaving," the other couples said. Those friends still talk about the faucet that seems to have a life of its own.

Later, Betts's sister Irene tried the tub faucet, and the sink faucet turned on. When Irene's husband, Jim, tried, nothing happened. "Jim's a Yankee," says Irene. But Betts's mystified friends were all Southerners. Only Betts and Irene, tied to Miss Clarissa through family, have the bizarre effect on the faucet.

Although the plumbing made for engaging conversation and intriguing party games, Betts worried she had serious problems with the system. "My plumber checked with one of the head fellows at the Chattanooga Water Department to see if he'd ever heard of such a thing. He hadn't. Other plumbers came out, and they could not figure out why the sink kept turning on by itself."

Betts and Charlie are not concerned about the angry spirit. They have crafted a life with their two sons that is everything they ever hoped for. And besides, Miss Clarissa's firm hand protects them from harm. Betts has always been aware of her nurturing presence and feels a strong bond with her.

"I love Miss Clarissa. I love her spunkiness, the fact that she continued to keep that farm together after she lost her husband, even through the Civil War. I don't know if I'd call her a ghost, but there's definitely a spirit there. I talk to her all the time. When I'm cleaning, we talk about the house. She never talks back," Betts says, laughing.

Many people would say that Betts is much like Miss Clarissa, drawing from a deep spiritual well. She farms the land worked by generations before her and has served as president of the Georgia Cattleman's Association. She's an ardent participant in the political process, and she's spunky, too. Most of all, she cherishes her family and the house that shelters it.

"This house is such a treasure to me. But sometimes in a storm, when the wind is blowing really hard and the trees are blowing back and forth, it's a little spooky. Then I say, *Okay, this house has stood since the 1830s.* That gives me a little bit of comfort. Maybe the spirits who have lived here before are taking care of it."

They're taking care of the Berrys, too, despite at least one very cranky Yankee.

little house of spirits

CHICKAMAUGA, GEORGIA

*Do some places, normal in every other way, act as ragged
tears in time, allowing the past to intrude upon the present
in unexpected and uninvited ways? The Jackson place
seems to be a supernatural portal where diverse and drift-
ing spirits come and go. Some even venture from the corner lot on Clebourne Avenue, tagging along with the family around town.*

A home like the Jacksons' in downtown Chickamauga is
the last place most living souls would expect to encounter
otherworldly houseguests. The modest one-story ranch house
with a low-pitched roof, a full basement, and an attached
garage typifies many homes built in 1967. It boasts a shaded
front patio on which any Southerner would enjoy drinking
iced tea while reposing in wicker and watching neighbors
come and go. There, Mrs. Billy Jackson sinks into pink floral
cushions and motions for Sophie the poodle to jump on her
lap. She begins her story.

Sophie listens as Mrs. Jackson tells of the many entities that clatter about their home.

Several months after moving in, Mrs. Jackson came home one afternoon to find buttermilk splattered all over her kitchen cabinets. It appeared someone had just tossed it into the air. She fussed at her teenager, Pam, for such carelessness. Pam denied it. It wasn't the sort of thing her daughter would do, but Mrs. Jackson didn't know what else to make of it.

Soon afterward, Mrs. Jackson returned home and found a green ink stain on her kitchen carpet. Again, she blamed Pam. Again, Pam denied it. She claimed she didn't own any green ink—or indeed any ink at all. Mrs. Jackson had to concede that.

The kitchen and the refrigerator in particular seemed a gateway to another dimension. While preparing dinner, Mrs. Jackson heard a small voice talking there. But she couldn't make out what the invisible child was saying. "What?" she asked several times. Each time, the child repeated what sounded like gibberish. Mrs. Jackson was unable to understand what the child wanted.

Later, thirteen-year-old Pam saw a man at the refrigerator. She thought he looked like a neighbor—until he disappeared before her eyes. She said nothing to her mother. But from then on, she feared coming home to the empty house after school without at least one friend with her.

One evening, Mrs. Jackson's son-in-law came home late from an outing with friends and went downstairs. He told Pam, "Well, you're down here. How did you get down here so fast? You were upstairs when I came in."

Pam insisted she wasn't.

"Yeah, you were," he argued. "I asked you if you were mad at me, and you said no."

She still denied she had seen him come in.

"Come to think about it, you walked right into the refrigerator."

Later, the son-in-law had the opportunity to witness the odd shenanigans again. While in the living room, he heard a loud clatter. He found the curtains had crashed down in Mr. Jackson's room. Mrs. Jackson went to the hardware store, bought some sturdy metal reinforcements, and remounted the curtains. "It wasn't long 'til down they come again. He broke them, just broke them in half," she says.

Mrs. Jackson's mother became worried when she phoned the house and someone picked up but didn't speak. Concerned that a family member was hurt or sick, she and her granddaughter hurried over to check. No one was home. The kitchen phone was off the hook, lying on a barstool. "That just scared her to death," Mrs. Jackson says. "She thought somebody was in the house."

Another time while visiting, her mother witnessed a female ghost—perhaps the one the son-in-law had seen walking into the refrigerator. "She thought it was me walking across the front of the house," Mrs. Jackson says. But she wasn't even home at the time.

The invisible occupant found ways to keep Mrs. Jackson out of the lower and back areas of the house. When she sewed in the basement, "he would tear up the machine or get upstairs, stomp, bang, carry on—do something to get me out from down there." When she worked in the backyard, "he'd get in the house and tear up something. He tore my curtains down and wall sconces in here."

Mrs. Jackson started seeing shadows moving about the house. But there were no people attached to them. She also began to hear noises—knocking, slamming, scraping, footsteps, and other sounds—from unoccupied rooms and hallways.

She became curious about a particular scraping and banging sound she heard regularly. One day while making up the brass bed, she pushed it against the wall. She had found the source of the sound. But what or who *caused* it?

An unseen force occupied the bedroom. Sometimes, "they'd set on my bed, but I couldn't see them," she says. One night, something or someone "grabbed me on the knee and squeezed."

The uninvited houseguests had become a bit too cozy for the Jacksons. They were about to get even more intimate.

"That ghost went to the hospital with me," Pam told her mother when she returned home from surgery one year. "It aggravated me, and finally I told him to get out because I was having surgery the next morning, and I didn't want him there."

When Mrs. Jackson was admitted to Tri-County Hospital in Fort Oglethorpe, the entity accompanied her, too. "When I checked in the hospital that night, he was in the closet. I thought it was somebody in the next room." Then she heard sheets rustling at the foot of her bed. Pam was sound asleep on a sofa, and Mrs. Jackson's own sheets were intact. "So I raised up and looked, and sure enough, there was a sheet wadded up at the foot of my bed."

He also tagged along to her next surgery. A ficus plant in the room was "just rattling," waking her up. Mrs. Jackson at first thought it was a strong air-conditioning current. But since it was October, both the heat and air were off.

The ghost seemed to take an interest in the most mundane activities. When Mrs. Jackson dropped in to see her mother, the older woman quit her bathroom cleaning to chat with her daughter. "I was just in there for a minute," Mrs. Jackson says. When her mother returned to the task after her daughter left, nothing could be found of the cleaning supplies, despite a thorough search. She had to buy more.

Quite the man about town, the ghost went with Mrs. Jackson to have her hair done.

Stylist Mary Brown, who lives in Chattanooga Valley, confessed that there was a ghost in her own mother's home. "It'd be fun to have one," she told Mrs. Jackson.

"Mine goes with me, so I'll bring him over here," Mrs. Jackson said.

The next Friday, as Mrs. Jackson was leaving the house for Mrs. Brown's, she told the ghost, "Come on. Mary wants you to come over and stay a week with her. If you're here, just come on and go with me."

She arrived at Mrs. Brown's for her standing appointment. "I told him to come on over here, that you wanted him. I don't know whether he's at the house or not. I haven't heard anything." She had her hair done and left.

The following Friday, "the minute I walked in the door," Mrs. Jackson says, "she told me to take that thing home with me. 'My husband hasn't slept a wink this week. That ghost has slammed and banged all week long.'"

The entity returned home with Mrs. Jackson. "As far as I know, he hasn't gone back over there," she says.

The peculiar activity ceased when Mr. Jackson came home from his long trips as a truckdriver. Only once, home alone, did he hear the banging and clanking so familiar to his wife and daughter. Since Mr. Jackson retired and is home all week, says Mrs. Jackson, "there's not that much a-happening."

Though Mrs. Jackson would occasionally bump into an invisible person while raking the front yard, it seemed for a while that the agitated spirits had left her in peace. Until May 2003. While washing her car in the driveway, she was surprised to see two Confederate soldiers standing on the other side of the vehicle. They looked right at her and then almost instantly faded out. "They were filthy dirty, like they'd been sleeping in the woods for several days." Sporting untidy brown beards and wearing heavy jackets and little "hats like you see in pictures," they had weapons hanging from their wide belts.

A psychic had told her years earlier about the two soldiers, and a friend had once said a soldier had hollered and waved at her from the Jacksons' yard. Mrs. Jackson had figured it was a reenactor, although why he'd be hanging out in a subdivision was anybody's guess. The psychic had noted the soldiers "loved [the] goldfish pond" in the front yard. Nonetheless, their appearance caught Mrs. Jackson off guard. Why did the apparitions suddenly materialize thirty-six years after the home's construction?

She was still puzzling over the two soldiers when, about thirty minutes later, she saw a woman cut across the edge of her yard and walk down the street. She wore a "long denim dress with long sleeves [and] a bonnet with a big brim, and [she] carried a big ol' wicker basket with a handle on it." Mrs. Jackson did not see what the woman had in her basket before she, too, vanished.

Despite its agreeable and inviting small-town façade, the little house on the corner seems to be a doorway to another world. Nearby homes of similar vintage have also experienced peculiar noises and strange occurrences. Perhaps the common element is that the ground they sit on has been inhabited on and off for centuries.

Just down the hill is Crawfish Springs, where a Cherokee courthouse once stood briefly in the 1820s. According to Mrs. Ruth Lee, writing in the early part of the twentieth century, despite the clear springs and rich land, the Cherokees did not thickly settle the area, fearing it cursed or even haunted by the previous occupants, unknown and mysterious to the Cherokees.

This nameless tribe had built mounds before disappearing, possibly decimated by a sudden outbreak of disease. Only the eerie legend of their passing remains.

Later, the Gordon Lee Mansion was built across the street from the springs. The mansion was once the heart of a twenty-five-hundred-acre plantation that encompassed the Jacksons' neighborhood. The caretaker, a Cherokee man, lived alone in a small cabin near the Jackson property and chased trespassers away. He was said to spend days at a time inside a mysterious cave in what is now the Jacksons' backyard. Is this cave the source of Mrs. Jackson's otherworldly visitors?

"I've never been in that cave, and I don't ever plan on going in it," she says. But she will show it to visitors. The poodle is not interested. She stays curled up on the front porch.

Descending into the backyard, Mrs. Jackson stops short where the ground drops abruptly into a huge gap in the landscape. She lights a cigarette. Despite the bright sky, peering down the steep bank is like looking into a dark pit. A layer of dead leaves from the surrounding large oaks litters the bowl-shaped depression. Lying close to the Jacksons' line, the cave entrance has been covered with tree limbs the neighbors helped pile up in hopes of sealing it.

Many cultures believe caves are portals to other worlds. Small, immortal creatures possessing mystical powers—such as fairies in Europe and the Little People of Cherokee lore—often inhabit them. Little People can be mischievous and don't appreciate trespassers. Although fiercely protective of their piece of earth, they are known to help lost humans, especially young ones. Who would be more lost than boys killed in battle, miles away from home?

The Battle of Chickamauga spilled over the neighborhood in 1863. Both Union and Confederate troops used the Gordon Lee Mansion and several other nearby sites as hospitals. Cannon fire was exchanged. Every place reeked of death and mutilation. To the north, men, horses, and farm animals littered the fields and forests, the victims of relentless artillery fire and a hail of bullets. Many wounded crawled off to hide and pray, hoping to live long enough to see the end of the day—or to just die in peace.

It is impossible to know exactly what transpired on the Jackson property. Though no grand battle took place there, it is within three miles of where the major action occurred. The suffering, shock, and dread men experienced practically within hollering distance can only be surmised. But the spirits of the cave know. Have they created a safe haven at the Jackson home that attracts the lost of Chickamauga? Do they play tricks on Mrs. Jackson for building over their cave? Or do they speak gibberish to her in the kitchen, believing her a kind and kindred spirit?

The many energies trapped on Clebourne Avenue may still be seeking in death the refuge they once so desperately needed in life. They may tarry awhile yet, for Mrs. Jackson is a sympathetic and understanding woman.

Tom and Ruth Lee (back) are part of the family, say the Forresters (Cory, Laura, Kirby, and Dale, front, left to right).
Photo of Lees courtesy of Dale Forrester.

the family that stayed

CHICKAMAUGA, GEORGIA

It would seem ghosts are trapped, unable to leave the earthly plane and move on, yet always longing to. But can a home and the lives lived there be so inviting, so enticing, that spirits just won't go? The Tom Lee House in Chickamauga may be such an enchanted place. For over a hundred years, the old house has nurtured three generations of a close family. It seems some members have decided to stay. Indefinitely.

The wrought-iron gate off Lee Avenue in Chickamauga swings open to a walkway leading gently up through ancient oaks to a white house roofed in green. Built in the mid-1890s by newlyweds Tom and Ruth Lee, the residence is one of the five oldest in town. The home's history has been a happy one.

A center of social activity, the house welcomed countless visitors over the decades. Wedding receptions and dances were often held there, attended by the many friends of the family and hosted by Mrs. Lee, the epitome of Southern grace and hospitality.

One hundred years later, the new mistress of the house, Laura Forrester, follows in Mrs. Lee's footsteps as a warm and gracious hostess. She shares with her husband, Dale, a keen interest in the home's history. They enjoy relating the stories of the three generations who lived there before them and who, they believe, may still be sharing the rooms and hallways.

Tom Lee was Congressman Gordon Lee's younger brother, explains Dale. He was close to his older sibling yet always in his shadow. However, his wealth meant that the Emory-educated lawyer did not have to compete with his brother or anyone else. "He had tried his first case, and it was scotch," Dale chuckles. "He liked it so much better, he never did anything else."

A friendly man, Tom was always out and about chatting with neighbors and shopkeepers. "He liked to walk around town wearing a suit," says Laura. He was the town's first school superintendent and was instrumental in local politics.

His attraction to Ruth was destined. "She was very jovial, a very funny woman," Dale says. They had a wonderful marriage. After fifty-eight years together, they died in the same year—1949. They were buried together behind First Baptist Church down the street.

Since they never had children, they left the house to their favorite niece, Mary Henderson, who lived next door with her husband, Fred. The Forresters discovered the Hendersons' 1914 wedding-guest book—complete with pressed flowers and rice—in the attic. Mary and Fred moved into the house shortly after the deaths of the Lees. Their kids were already grown when they settled in, so the home remained childless.

One evening in 1963, Fred returned from a fishing trip.

While cleaning his catch on the back porch, he had a heart attack and died. His body lay in state in the sitting room. After forty-nine years of marriage, Mary found herself a widow in a large house with only memories to keep her company. She passed away in the mid-1970s, leaving the house to her daughter, Mary Hill, who, like her parents before her, lived next door with her husband. Their children, too, were already grown. Mrs. Hill lived in the Tom Lee House until her death in 1995. The heirs then decided to sell the home that had nurtured their family for an entire century.

The Forresters bought the Tom Lee House in the spring of 1997, becoming the first people to live there who are not family members. With them came children—the first ever to inhabit the house. Peculiar things started happening right away.

Dale was the first to sense a supernatural presence in the home. Looking through some boxes in the attic, he found Tom and Ruth's photo. His flashlight went off, then on, then off and on again before finally dying. He couldn't see a thing in the pitch-black attic. It was dark outside, too. He hadn't realized he had been there so long. Where had the time gone? He experienced the eerie feeling that he wasn't alone. "I was spooked. I flew out of there," he says.

Dale Forrester was surprised to find this old photo of Mary Hill on a pony in "Aunt Ruth's yard."

Laura's first encounter came when she had a sense that a shadow was moving across the sitting room toward the bookcase. She didn't say anything about it for a long time. One evening, she and Dale were talking in the living room when the shadow again caught her eye. She kept talking.

"What did you see?" Dale asked.

"Do you ever see—" Laura began.

"—a shadow that goes across there?" he interrupted, pointing toward the sitting room. Dale confessed he'd been seeing it for a long time. They could witness it from another room, too.

"It's just a shadow, and I wouldn't say that it's a figure, but it's enough to catch your attention," says Laura. The shadow offers no clue to its identity or purpose.

But the ghost of Fred Henderson makes his presence and intentions quite clear. He thinks the Forresters spend too much money on heat. "I'll have the thermostat on seventy-eight because the house is very hard to heat," says Laura. "I'll start getting cold and look at the thermostat. It's on seventy. I'll turn it back, and in a little while the same thing will happen." This always occurs when Laura is alone.

"If somebody's turning the thermostat down, we think that it's Fred," says Laura. "A lady who used to do Mary Henderson's hair told us that [Mary] would get really mad at Fred because she would try to warm the house up and he would come back behind her and turn the thermostat down. They were very frugal. Everyone around town knew that."

The Forresters had the thermostat checked. Nothing was wrong with it.

Other events continue to keep the family mystified. "That secretary used to be in the next room. That red-and-white plate was on it," Laura says, pointing to a reproduction Johnson Brothers transferware dish. "I'd walk through, and instead of facing forward, it'd be turned sideways. I'd flip it around, come back in a little while, and it was sideways again."

She turned it several times before she began to wonder why it was constantly out of place. Dale had also noticed and straightened the wayward plate. They discovered they'd both been rotating it a lot, and neither had told the other. They decided to move the plate to a small table in the next room. Someone was pleased with the new location and let it be.

Laura had a more personal contact with an unseen resident. Fixing dinner in the kitchen with her back to the door, she felt someone pat her on the fanny. She turned around to an empty room. She sensed it was a man's touch and assumed it was Dale. But Dale sat in another room watching television. "I knew he couldn't get from there to here in that time, but I walked in there and said, 'Did you just come in here and touch me on the bottom?' He said no. I said, 'Well, I just felt something do that.' "

Many days later, she was lying alone in bed with her back to the wall when she felt someone touch her fanny. "I thought it was my husband again. I turned over, thinking that he had come to bed. There was nobody there. For a few minutes, I was a little scared. I got up and came in the sitting room, and he had fallen asleep watching television on the sofa. My daughter was in her bed, and Corey was in his bed. When I saw that everybody was okay, I went back to bed and went to sleep. I've never felt really afraid."

Their children were not ignored by the spooky presence. An affable spirit communicated the pleasure of a long-ago birthday party to the Forresters' little girl, seemingly while the child slept.

"Kirby was five years old, about to turn six," says Dale. "One day, she says, 'Daddy, I want to have a birthday party, and I want to have a pony ride.' And that was odd because she'd never been near a pony in her life. We're not horse people. We thought that would pass—she's got three or four months before her birthday. A few days later, she comes out after waking up and says, 'I want to have a pony ride.' This goes on for several days. Finally, she says she wants to have all her friends over to ride, in the front yard. A few days later, she says the pony's going to be brown and white."

The family never had that party. But a couple of years later, Dale found another box in the attic containing photographs, one of which was a black-and-white of a young Mary Hill—who resided in the house as an adult but lived next door as a child—sitting astride a bicolored pony in front of what later became Kirby's bedroom window. On the back, the inscription said, "Aunt Ruth's yard." Dale now keeps the photo downstairs. "I have a whole series of these pictures—all these little girls taking turns riding the pony."

By the time Kirby was twelve or thirteen, visions of pony rides had long faded. Her next encounter was more direct—and, she felt, not friendly. One evening about ten or eleven o'clock, she had just settled into bed—the same bed Laura was in when the unseen hand touched her. "I went in there to check her," says Laura. "Usually, I kiss her and tell her good night. I don't remember if I did or not. I pulled the door to. I probably didn't get farther than partway through the adjoining room when she let out a bloodcurdling scream. By the time I got back in there, she was crying."

Laura's first instinct was to check for a spider or bee in the bed, since Kirby had been stung before. But Kirby had the covers pulled up. "Somebody grabbed me," she told her mother.

Laura assured her no one was there. "Nobody can grab you."

"I don't care. Somebody grabbed me." She wanted her mother to look under the bed.

Laura knew the storage boxes under the bed would allow no room for a person, but she checked anyway. "And I looked in the closet," Laura says. "Nobody's there."

Did Kirby have a bad dream? Laura says no. Kirby was awake when Laura had left her seconds before the incident.

Laura speculates maybe it was Ruth tucking Kirby in. "She obviously loved her niece and let children have parties here. Did I forget to tuck her in? Maybe Ruth came along behind me."

Kirby is not so sure. "It felt like someone on the bed beside me, shoving me. It didn't feel like it was friendly."

Fifteen-year-old big brother had a run-in with a pushy and uninvited roommate, too. Corey sleeps in a portion of the attic converted for him. "I was up in my room recently," he says. "I got in my bed and was watching television. I pulled the covers over me and turned to the side. All of a sudden, I hear something like a door opening—the attic door. I remained calm but kinda nervous because no one else should be up there. All of a sudden, I felt the right side of the bed sink a little bit. I'm thinking, *Oh, my gosh.* I pulled the covers up over my face a little bit, still watching TV, and I feel someone just reach around like they were trying to put their arms around me, trying to strangle me. I am sweating. I'm about to have a panic attack—I'm terrified! Then they were poking me or something. It didn't really hurt, but it was tight. They grabbed me hard. I can't explain it. It was weird."

Being alone in his corner of the house, he had few options. In desperation, he counted to himself—*One, two, three*—then screamed at the intruder. When he peeked out, the door was closed. No one was there.

Other times, the door *would* be open. Laura would go upstairs and see it open and the light on. She'd fuss at Corey and ask what he'd been doing in there. "I haven't been in the attic," he would protest.

If the Forrester family suffers from hysteria, it's contagious. Dale bought a big-screen television in 2001. "He couldn't watch anything on it until the cable was connected," says Laura, "so the cable guy came out and went down to the cellar." The cellar is open and bright, explains Laura. She's never been frightened by it in the least.

Dale came home that night and turned on the television. It didn't respond. He stomped down to the cellar and inspected the cable work. It was a dreadful job. "There was cable everywhere," says Dale, waving his hands. It was no wonder the television wouldn't work. So the Forresters called and complained.

A cable-company representative came out and apologized to the family for the technician's speedy retreat. "He got scared in your cellar, said he saw something and felt something," the cable man told Laura. "He ran out and got in the truck and radioed in, 'You'll have to send somebody else to finish that job. I will *never* go back to that house.'"

And he didn't. Another man finished the job without incident—or at least not that he'd admit to.

When the Forresters brought a rescued poodle into the family, the ghostly activities ceased for several months. The family was lulled into thinking that the strange energies of the house had finally played out. But they were only slumbering. Without warning, the ghost that had earlier grabbed Corey returned, signaling that the supernatural forces were awakening once more.

While watching television at about two o'clock in the morning in his attic hideaway, Corey, by this time a Gordon Lee High School senior, heard footsteps climbing the stairs. *Maybe it's squirrels in the roof*, he thought. But the steps kept coming, clear and even, toward him. *Maybe it's Mom coming to check on me*, he thought. So he looked to see. "There's a dude walking up my stairs," he recalls. Corey saw what appeared to be a flesh-and-blood fellow about his own age, slender, tanned, and blond, wearing overalls and no shirt. Corey pulled the covers over his face. The footsteps kept coming. Corey tried to flatten himself under the covers in the hope that he wouldn't be seen. Then the steps stopped. Corey, barely breathing, began to shake.

"All of a sudden, I felt my bed sink in like somebody just

put their knees up on there. He lays on my back and I can't breathe, my chest is just so heavy." There was no doubt in Corey's mind that someone was crushing him. He struggled through three breaths before the ghost got up and walked away. Corey felt safe once more but perplexed. No one knows who the young man could have been. Perhaps he was a laborer who had lodged in the attic many decades ago.

Soon thereafter, someone developed an avid interest in the dining-room china cabinet. The family began to find one door open. No one would admit to leaving it that way. One day, Corey and his friend Jared came through the dining room past the open door. "Miss Laura," Jared asked, "did you open this door?" Laura assured him that she had not. The boys closed and locked it. Then, as they watched, the brass key turned completely back and unlocked the cabinet. Laura, taking her cue from the two bloodless faces, asked the boys if they had seen the key move. "Yes, ma'am," said Jared. "I saw the key turn."

Those who loved the house for three generations must still be there, sharing it with the Forresters. But even they may be spooked occasionally by an earlier generation of earthbound spirits. The yard was once part of an outdoor morgue. "We were told," Dale says, "that when they were using the Gordon Lee Mansion as a hospital during the battle [of Chickamauga], there were bodies laid on our property." In the 1970s, experts found cannonballs and other evidence of combat in the Forresters' yard. It is well known that what is now downtown Chickamauga was nearly engulfed in one of the bloodiest battles of the Civil War.

But the Forresters still feel safe and content in the Tom Lee House. "I never felt at home in our first house, and we built that house," says Laura. "The very first night we moved in here, I felt good, that we belonged here."

Several previous generations feel the same way. Even now.

the haunted doorway

CHICKAMAUGA, GEORGIA

What does an earthbound spirit do when the object of his longing is taken apart and taken away? Is it really a house that keeps him, or is it a certain knob, or a mantel, or the creaking floorboards he walked in life? Or a special doorway through which he still seeks dear memories? Some ghosts stay with the land, others the home, and still others just pieces of what was once a home.

Irene Jewell Staub had just graduated from the University of Georgia, class of 1975. She was keen to take on adult responsibilities and the independence that went with them. But by no means was she going far from her girlhood home of Chickamauga. Her Southern values held her to family, place, and tradition like buttermilk stuck to the side of a glass. She had already landed her first job—teaching first- and second-graders at Rock Springs Elementary—and was eager to set up housekeeping nearby.

Irene's grandmother Hall owned a broken row of rental houses on Elder Alley, just blocks away from her own home. They were modest in size but endowed with architectural tidbits unusual for mill workers' bungalows. They boasted fine pine floors, hard and solid, and trim more detailed than you might expect, with rosettes over the doors.

Irene and her grandmother spent that summer redoing one of the houses. They sawed and nailed and painted and polished until the old cottage came to life again. Before the leaves turned, Irene, filled with excitement, moved in. She and the little house seemed perfect for each other.

About three weeks later, she awoke late at night, sensing someone in the room. To her horror, she saw a man standing in the doorway, just watching her. He was tall and slim and wore a "solid-black old-timey suit," she recalls. Irene screamed and reached for the light. There was no one there. Thinking she was dreaming, she sank uneasily back into her pillows and drifted off.

She saw him again three or four weeks later—same time, same clothing, standing in the same doorway. "His dress was not of this era," she emphasizes. This happened seven or eight times from September through April. "It was midnight, always midnight," she says.

One midnight, the ghost walked toward a terrified Irene.

She told her friends, family, and colleagues at school about the eerie visitor.

"Were you dreaming, or do you think it was a real ghost?" they asked, intrigued.

"Oh, I don't know," she answered, and they all laughed about it.

But I was awake, she told herself.

In April, Irene stayed up late preparing for a visit by school accreditation officials. "I had not been asleep maybe ten minutes. I felt like somebody was in the room," she says. This time, the spooky figure approached closer and closer, stopping at her bed. Irene had never felt threatened before. "I screamed, turned the light on, and lay in bed, too frightened to get up, for about ten to fifteen minutes." Finally, she slipped out of bed, checked the bathroom, then called her brother Bryan to come spend the rest of the night with her.

The next morning, Irene went to school.

"What is wrong with you?" asked the first person she saw. "You're so pale, you look like you've seen a ghost."

Irene burst into tears and replied in a broken whimper, "I think I did see a ghost."

She suffered such distress that she couldn't sleep in her house for about two months. "I'd come home, do whatever I needed to do there, then come over and spend the night with Grandmother Hall."

Irene went on a trip. When she returned, she felt calmer. But she was still rattled about the uninvited man in her house, so she visited a Presbyterian minister in Dalton, Georgia, who counseled people who'd seen apparitions. He immediately asked Irene how she knew she wasn't asleep.

"I really don't know," she told him. "But I do know that whatever happened to me scared me so badly that I haven't been able to sleep in my house for a couple of months."

"What are you most afraid of?"

"Death."

"In all the years I've worked with people who've seen apparitions, none of the apparitions has ever killed anybody." The minister suggested she keep a pad and pencil by her bed and make a mark when she saw the ghost to prove she was awake. She also rearranged her bedroom furniture.

The ghost didn't reappear for almost a year. When Irene did see him again, she screamed and turned the light on but saw no one, as always.

Another year went by. She was up late one hot July night working on her master's degree. Since she had no air conditioning, she had left her windows and front door open but had locked her screen door. She had just fallen into bed. Midnight loomed near.

Then she saw him. She panicked and ran right through the ghostly figure. She reached the dining room and turned the light on. He was gone.

Irene remembered she'd left the front door open. She slammed it, locked it, got back into bed, and pulled the covers over her. "There was a knock at my door," she says. "I ignored it. The knock was more insistent. I continued to ignore it. Then, when it became really loud, I heard someone yelling my name. I got up and went to the front door."

"Who is it?" Irene squeaked.

To her relief, her neighbor answered, "It's Mrs. Plaster." Mrs. Plaster had just gone to bed when she heard a scream and a slamming door. Although almost eighty, she found her way across the darkened gravel driveway to Irene's door. "What on earth is wrong? I was scared. I thought someone had grabbed you."

"You're going to think I'm so silly. I think I have a ghost in this house." Irene felt sheepish.

About that time, the Chickamauga police drove up in front of the house. Mrs. Plaster waved them on. The kind old woman then calmed the panicked Irene. "No, I don't think you're silly. Strange things have happened to me over the years, and some strange things happened to my neighbor on the other side of me. Her house burned long before you moved here. Someone would knock on their front door, and they'd go answer it, and nobody'd be there. Then they'd hear a knock on the back door, and nobody'd be there either." Quite a few times over the years, Mrs. Plaster had felt that somebody was in *her* house, too.

"After that, I never saw him again," Irene says. "It happened the first four years I was there, then no more."

Who was the mysterious figure in Irene's bedroom doorway? One of the careworn working-class tenants who had lived there over the decades? Perhaps. If so, he will remain a mystery, as such people are seldom commented about in local papers and letters and thus pass on unnoticed.

The alert Mrs. Plaster may have come closest to the truth. "All these houses are made from the same wood," she told Irene that night in the driveway.

And the wood wasn't new. It was once part of the grand Kensington Hotel. The five-story hotel was the crown jewel of an ambitious plan by a Pennsylvania land speculator to create a thriving town in rural Walker County in 1890. Boasting that the project carried no debt and no mortgage, the optimistic F. R. Pemberton built the city, then began efforts to populate it. "We have plenty of money—all we need is people," he told the *Chattanooga Daily Times*. The newspaper devoted two large articles to the planned town, raving shamelessly about its splendor and potential. It seemed that outsiders had come to north Georgia and discovered utopia.

Three years later, the bubble burst. The *Walker County Messenger* began running ads for the dispersal of the hotel, forty new cottages, land, and other assets. Sometime after 1915, the top two floors of the hotel were demolished. It was probably one of Irene's great-grandfathers, Dr. Elder, who bought the lumber. Around 1930, it was likely used in the construction of a group of sturdy little well-trimmed homes on small lots. "When I first moved there," Irene recalls, "there were only four houses. But there had been more once. Over the years, some had burned."

Today, only two houses remain, including the one Irene once lived in. They are surrounded by more modern homes lining a little street now known as Elder Avenue. Irene inherited her grandmother's large house several blocks away and lives there with her husband and three boys. She has encountered no otherworldly residents within its welcoming walls.

More than twenty-five years have gone by since Irene's ghostly encounters. "At that time, I would have sworn it was real," she says. "Then, as time goes on, you wonder, *Did I just have a reoccurring dream, month after month, for almost a year? And then again over the next three years?* I could've sworn it was a very real experience. I always wondered why he never came back."

Why did the ghostly figure lurk there to begin with? Why did he peer through the doorway at Irene? Did he see Irene or someone else, maybe his own wife, waiting for him? Or was he an attentive father silently watching over a beloved daughter?

Perhaps he was just a man who had lost everything in a turn-of-the-twentieth-century land rush, clinging to one small piece of a once-large dream.

the general's rocker

TUNNEL HILL, GEORGIA

The inability to accept defeat keeps many spirits earth-bound. Confederate general John Bell Hood is among those at Tunnel Hill who cannot leave. He lost twice—in love and war.

Something unexpected, almost secret, lies beneath Chetoogeta Mountain in a sleepy corner of northern Whitfield County. A deserted tunnel hewn decades ago remains, a monument to the will of men past and present. The dark passageway invites talk of ghosts. It is forbidding, cold, and murky, even with the lights on. Walking through its 1,744 feet of endless bricks gives a person a sense of stepping into another world, one where humans are interlopers.

The tunnel's history is as dark as its interior. Death and tragedy visited it before the rails were even hammered down. Burrowing through rock is dangerous. Some workers—including the Irish laborers who laid its brick lining in an old

Irish pattern—left the site in crude coffins. Even now, strains of old Irish songs drift from the shadows.

The tunnel was finished on Halloween 1849. The great celebration included the breaking of six bottles of spirits against its walls. For the next thirteen years, this shortcut through the mountain pumped the lifeblood of commerce into the regional economy. It provided the shortest route to Dalton by foot or buggy, says local historian Larry Thornton. People, wagons, and trains passed through regularly.

Its value as an artery of transport attracted attention as the War Between the States drew closer. Any means of moving the wares of war—including food, supplies, and men—was valuable. During the war, Larry says, traffic through the tunnel tripled. War refugees fleeing north or south passed through it every day, as did local people running errands. The most famous travelers were the Yankee spies Andrews' Raiders, known for their role in "the Great Locomotive Chase." An engine called "the General," stolen by Andrews' Raiders at Kennesaw, roared through the tunnel in 1862 to escape the engine Texas, in hot pursuit, before finally being captured above Ringgold.

Both sides saw the tunnel as a strategic asset. They fought over it in one skirmish after another, kicking and biting like two old mares after a bucket of oats. For two years, men killed and died all around the tunnel, some becoming the lost souls who still haunt it today.

Not surprisingly, Larry knows more eerie tales about the tunnel and the men who fought for it than you can shake a stick at. He doesn't believe in ghosts but admits that the yarns about the bloody ground are replete with curious twists. It is common, he says, to see spirits in the tunnel—often several men who appear in the evening or morning mist. "Some say they are Confederate soldiers from one of the many winter camps," he says. They may also be the shades of tunnel workers. "The dress in the period would fit either one, as the Confederate uniforms were of part gray or tan homespun and slouch hats."

Confederate lieutenant general John Bell Hood is the highest-ranking haint at Tunnel Hill. When he arrived there on September 21, 1863, he was in no condition to fight, having been shipped in among an overflow of wounded Confederate men and officers from the fierce fighting at Chickamauga. The hospital "was a forerunner of a MASH," says registered nurse and reenactor Kimberlee Bruce. "It was also a convalescent hospital, so they got them from Shiloh, Nashville, and Murfreesboro." Men injured in battle miles away sometimes drew their last breath within sight and sound of the tunnel.

General Hood was billeted in the Clisby Austin House several hundred feet west of the tunnel. In the thick of battle at Chickamauga, a minié ball had pierced his thigh. Less than three months earlier, in July 1863, he had taken a bullet in Gettysburg that shattered his left arm, leaving it useless. Larry believes that eminent physician T. G. Richardson amputated the general's right leg in the Clisby Austin House rather than at Chickamauga, as some historians say. The leg was buried in the Austin family cemetery within sight of the room where Hood was recuperating on a rope bed. It was thought that Hood would soon be reunited with his leg, so severe were the wound and the surgery that removed the limb.

A tall, rugged man with a booming voice, Hood was loved by his men. Some called him courageous, while others thought him reckless. Despite rumors that he had perished, Hood pulled through, thanks to his legendary determination. He left Tunnel Hill for Colonel Frank Little's home in the West Armurchee Valley to convalesce. When word came in late October that the Yankee cavalry was going to sweep down from Chattanooga and grab him, explains Larry, the

Confederates moved him under cover of night. Twelve slaves, working in shifts of six at a time, carried him by stretcher all the way from Armurchee back to Tunnel Hill, trotting down a dark road while singing "corn songs." "Hood, being on laudanum [an opiate], was real happy anyway," Larry says. "He just loved to hear those songs."

Hood also had fond memories of vivacious nineteen-year-old South Carolina belle Sally "Buck" Preston to keep him warm. Hood recalled the dreary morn in March 1862 when he first laid eyes on Buck. He fell hard, like a mule hit in the head with a fence post. "She stands on her feet like a thoroughbred," he told a friend. Hood later confided that he "surrendered to Buck at first sight." He wasn't alone. Men found her astoundingly attractive in bearing and form. Her hair was richly auburn, her eyes a changeable blue, her complexion milky smooth.

He was engaged to Buck—maybe. She dizzied him with her answers to his proposal, changing her mind more often than a cat poised in a doorway. When Hood declared himself engaged to her, she retorted, "I am not engaged to you." Yet she did not protest when the local paper later sensationalized the rumor of their engagement.

Buck returned Hood's affections, to a point. She flirted with him like she did with all men. It was said she could not help herself. Men would die for Hood, but Buck could no more be pinned down than a morning mist. His courage was of little use to him in his battle for Buck's hand. The coarse Hood was considered an unsuitable match for such a refined and splendid woman. Buck's pedigree was impeccable. Educated in Europe, she sat a horse so well that French emperor Napoleon III commended her. Thought to be the inspiration for Margaret Mitchell's Scarlett O'Hara, she was one of the South's most sought-after young ladies. Suitors circled her like moths helplessly charging a flame. She lost many admirers to the war. Even her beloved brother met death in battle. Was she bad luck? Despite the two crippling injuries he suffered after committing his heart to Buck, Hood didn't care if she was.

Hood reconciled himself to his loss of limbs, history says. During his convalescence, he dwelled on his men, the future of the cause, and no doubt Buck. When Hood was returned by litter to Tunnel Hill, says Larry, he spent the night once more at the Clisby Austin House. He subsequently visited Dalton and Atlanta by train, then headed back toward Richmond, Virginia, to continue courting Buck. His infatuation was his undoing.

When he arrived in Richmond in November 1863, all were atwitter over the brave, wounded general. Everyone, President Jefferson Davis included, visited Hood and plied him with gifts and praise. Everyone except the Prestons. The general finally had himself carried to their home, where he found Buck near tears over his frailty.

Hood spent Christmas Eve with the Prestons. That evening, he and Buck crossed swords. Her parents' disapproval of her prospective marriage to Hood was likely what sparked the quarrel. The volatile relationship cooled again. The next day, Hood told a friend that his pursuit of Buck was "the hardest battle" he had ever fought in his life.

The following February, Hood was promoted to lieutenant general and assigned to Dalton, eleven miles south of Tunnel Hill. The severe winter of 1863-64 saw a break in major action as soldiers fought cold and hunger rather than each other. But Hood fought for Buck that winter, visiting her, then retreating when her parents and older sister joined forces to drive him from Buck's life.

The spring of 1864 found North and South getting riled up again. On May 7, fifty thousand Yankees pouring in from the north sparked the Battle of Tunnel Hill. Outnumbered, the Confederates withdrew. On May 9, General William T.

Sherman led his Union troops past Tunnel Hill and Dalton toward Atlanta. Hood, a corps commander under General Joe Johnston, challenged Sherman on several fronts but was in the end bested. After the disastrous Battle of Atlanta, the Army of Tennessee returned to make a stand in Dalton. Sherman turned his back on his rail supply line, abandoning the tunnel in favor of pillaging supplies. Georgia was doomed.

Routed in love and war, Hood, now commanding the Army of Tennessee, rode back through Tunnel Hill in late October 1864 on his way to Franklin and Nashville, where he would be trounced once more. The hero Hood became a villain. Wrote Confederate captain Samuel T. Foster, "The wails and cries of widows and orphans made at Franklin . . . will heat up the fires of the bottomless pit to burn the soul of General J. B. Hood for murdering their husbands and fathers."

Hood's success in leading small groups of men did not translate to high-level command. His military career was destroyed along with the Army of Tennessee. Perhaps Buck *was* bad luck.

Not a man to fall on his sword, Hood visited Buck once more during 1865 in North Carolina, where the Prestons had traveled to escape Sherman's advance. She formally broke the engagement and soon thereafter fled to Europe with her family. Hood rode off, hat in hand, to Texas and surrender. The war was over.

Hood never saw Buck again. Nor did he speak of her. She spoke of him, however, wistfully saying that she wished he had fought harder against her family's refusal and swept her away. She would have given up everything, she declared too late.

Two years later, Buck returned from Europe and married one of her earlier beaus. A year after that, Hood married. He fathered eleven children in New Orleans before succumbing to yellow fever in 1879. His shattered body, hastily buried, was later moved to Metairie Cemetery. His leg remained in the

The ghost of General John Bell Hood is said to rock in the upstairs bedroom of the Clisby Austin House at Tunnel Hill.

quiet patch of north Georgia ground at Tunnel Hill. Buck, only thirty-eight years old, died the next year.

The general has found his way once more to the Georgia hills, seeking solace at the Clisby Austin House. What draws him there? Some say Hood cannot bear to part with his severed leg. Yet he braved the separation well in life. Others wonder if Hood, knowing Sherman planned his March to the Sea at that very house, has drawn near in hopes, this time, of foiling the Union plan.

Most likely, unrequited love holds fast the old soldier, nursing his broken heart over his failure to win Buck and ever plotting to woo her back.

Whatever his reason, Hood still makes his way slowly across the floors of the Clisby Austin House with a deliberate but muffled thump and drag, thump and drag. But mostly, he just sits and rocks in the second-floor east-facing bedroom where he lay wounded—by love and bullets—many years before. The empty rocking chair often creaks in the vacant room. If someone moves it to another place, it eases its way back to the spot by the window, where it catches the rays of a new sun each day.

THE BATTLE TO SAVE TUNNEL HILL

In its day, the tunnel was an engineering marvel. Workers started at both ends and dug toward the middle. When the two crews met after a third of a mile of digging, they were off by only an inch and a half. "They did real good," says Larry Thornton, "because they tried that in New Jersey in the [1970s] with a laser, and they missed it by four foot."

After a new tunnel was built nearby in 1928, the old tunnel fell into dangerous disrepair. By the 1990s, development had nearly erased the trenches, rifle pits, and winter campsites that once scarred the ridge top, and with them the memory of brave men long gone. As at many Civil War battle sites, the rich history of Tunnel Hill was nearly lost.

The Tunnel Hill Historical Foundation came to the rescue. "We saved the tunnel about twelve years ago," Larry says. The railroad, having no use for it, was filling the tunnel with dirt. The foundation convinced it to give up its state lease. Georgia then donated the property to the city of Tunnel Hill, which in turn leased it to the foundation. "It's safe now," Larry vows.

Today, a mat of kudzu smothers the ridge on each side of the tunnel. The rails and crossties are long gone, but the foundation cleaned and repaired the crumbing masonry walls, bought some surrounding acreage, and built the Heritage Center to exhibit artifacts and provide a glimpse into what once was. Each September, to honor those who fought and fell there, the battle is reenacted by men in blue and gray.

Efforts continue to interpret and preserve the site. Somewhere east of the house near or within the Austin family graveyard, there is rumored to be a plank on which was carved, "Here lies the gallant Hood's leg." Larry is talking with landowner Kenneth Holcomb about exhuming it in hopes of matching the DNA to Hood's descendants. "Then we're going to mark it," he says.

tales from north alabama

cemetery playmate

STEVENSON, ALABAMA

Most people fear cemeteries. They feel a foreboding that the dead are not resting in peace. Or resting at all. Visitors worry that, instead of passing to Judgment, some souls cannot leave their wasting corpses and so cling desperately to the living as they pass by.

As a paranormal investigator, Rita LaGrow Strugula makes it a point to meet ghosts. And she's met quite a few. But she will never forget her first encounter, as a five-year-old in a small Minnesota town. She awoke one clammy summer night to the sounds of someone shuffling up and down the hall outside the room she shared with her slightly older brother. The labored footsteps seemed to stop right outside her door. She looked up and saw no one. Then the disembodied voice of an old woman barked, "You kids stay out of my piggy-bank money!"

"I liked to have jumped out of my skin," says Rita.

Big bother and Rita's parents slept on, unaware of the peeved spirit. But her rude awakening to the world of ghosts changed Rita's life. Over the next twenty-five years, she learned all she could about them by reading and listening. Ten years ago, she began to seek out close encounters of the third kind. She wanted to find ghosts, document ghosts, talk to ghosts.

Founder of the North Alabama Paranormal Research Society, Rita leaves no headstone unturned when it comes to hunting ghosts in upper Alabama. When asked where the most ghosts can be found, she answers without hesitation: "Just about anywhere you go in the town of Stevenson is active. I've been to three of the cemeteries there, and all three of them have activity."

But Talley Cemetery, northwest of the city off County Road 170, stands out even among these. It is one of the area's oldest burial grounds. The tired headstones—or at least those you can still read—date as far back as 1835. Crude stones mark many graves, and some may not be marked at all. Once-neat cedars tower like ragged scarecrows over rough ground pocked with the sinkholes of old graves. Many of those who tended the cemetery are now buried there themselves. Fewer and fewer people come each year to clip weeds and prune limbs.

"You go out there," says Rita, "and you never know what's going to happen. But something *will* happen."

She visits often, camera in hand, to document what the naked eye sometimes misses.

Late one afternoon in midwinter, Rita and two friends stood in the heart of the cemetery near a fallen tree. "We felt something like drops of rain falling on us, only we were not getting wet." The "drops" were invisible. Rita was perplexed. Out of curiosity, she pulled out a set of dowsing rods— commonly used to witch water—to seek out the source of the ghostly droplets.

Dowsing rods are easily fashioned out of coat hangers bent into the shape of an L. The dowser loosely holds the lower, shorter legs of the L, one in each hand, leaving the longer leg to point straight ahead until activated by that which the dowser seeks.

When Rita approached the downed tree, the rods began twirling wildly. "I moved away from the tree, and they quieted down. When I approached the tree a second time, the rods did absolutely nothing."

Rita knows how to converse with ghosts using rods. She asks questions, then watches the rods. When they cross over each other, the answer is yes. When they swing wide open, the answer is no. She wondered if the bizarre action of the rods was spirit-related, so she attempted to engage the presence, using the rods as a conduit. She asked aloud if the entity was buried in the cemetery.

Immediately, the rods crossed. *Yes.*

She told the entity to point in the direction it wanted her to go. Then, following the bearing of the rods, she began walking. Like a needle pulling thread through coarse cloth, the rods drew Rita through the broken rows of stone.

"We stopped right in front of a grave, and it just went crazy," she says.

A tiny ghost haunts the secluded Talley Cemetery in Stevenson, Alabama.

It was the burial place of a baby boy laid in his earthen crib in 1940. A small lamb was carved atop his heart-shaped stone, which stood several feet from a shagbark hickory. The inscription read, *Gone so soon.*

Rita asked the child if his mother was buried there, too.

The rods said no. The small boy was alone in the graveyard. A quick look through cemetery records later suggested that his relatives are resting in another graveyard across town.

Rita asked the tiny ghost where he was.

Through the rods, he pointed to a dead tree in the older section of the graveyard.

"Do you want me to play with you?" she asked.

He said yes. He wanted her to join him in the dead tree.

The cemetery grew dark, so Rita told the little boy she would have to be going. Even seasoned ghost hunters are wary of graveyards when the light leaves and the shadows stay. But Rita's friend Reen, curious about the child's strong attachment to Rita, paused to ask two more questions.

"Do you know Rita?" she asked him.

The rods crossed.

"Have you seen her here before?"

The rods crossed again.

Rita has searched for ghosts for years, finding them in places expected and unexpected. This time, one found her. Curiosity goes both ways.

wagon train

Places of great historical import often inspire reports of ghosts or other unexplainable phenomena. But what causes an encounter with the unknown when, indeed, nothing is known?

Betty grew up on Sand Mountain in northeastern Alabama, east of Ider and south of Flat Rock. County Road 771 passed by the homeplace, but traffic was light in the days when the roads were dirt and people didn't hurry so much.

Early one summer evening, seventeen-year-old Betty was primping for a date. Her parents were still at work, leaving her alone in the house. As was the custom before air conditioning, the windows were open to catch the breeze, so she wasn't surprised to hear horses outside. Because she had friends who rode, she went out on the porch to greet them as they passed. But there were no horses and no friends, only the quiet. "There was no sound except the birds," she says.

She went back in the house. A few minutes later, she heard the horses again.

"It sounded like horses pulling a wagon," she says. "They used to have wagon trains around there all the time in the summer. I walked out and was going to holler to the people who were on the train to see if they were my friends."

Again, she saw no one.

She knew it couldn't be the television. "Our television was torn up," says Betty. So she checked the radio. It was off. She didn't think it could be a neighbor, since no one lived nearby. A person would have to climb on the roof to see the closest neighbor's house.

She returned to her room and soon heard the horses a third time.

"It sounded like it was coming toward the house, toward me. It began to sound like watching an old Western, a wagon train. You could hear the wagons, you could hear the people hollering, the horses' harnesses rattling, people calling to the horses."

Then the clamor took on a frightening urgency. Unfriendly voices overcame those of the wagon train.

"You could hear the yelling and the whooping and all, like they were attacking," says Betty. "You could hear the wagons racing. It sounded like someone circling them, gunfire, and people screaming. And way off in the distance, I heard a bugle, like a cavalry troop. And all of a sudden, there was a high-pitched scream. Then silence. That was the end of it."

She heard the strange noises only when in the house. They always ceased when she went outside. Not wanting to hear the sounds again, she went into the yard and waited for her boyfriend to pick her up.

"I never talked to anybody about it," she says. If anyone else experienced it, they didn't talk either.

In 1862, Fort Donelson fell, leaving Alabama easy pickings for Yankee troops. No famous battles were fought in that neck of the woods. But Sand Mountain was just a hop, skip, and jump from the major action in Chattanooga and Chickamauga. Federal troops moved through the area, using routes just west of Ider. And wherever troops moved, wagons moved with them, carrying supplies.

Because most northeastern Alabama boys were quick to sign up for the Rebel army, they had almost all been assigned elsewhere—mostly to General Joe Johnston's army—by the time the Yankees came tramping through Alabama. The few Confederate troops left were deemed guerrillas by the Yankees and were treated as such if captured.

Both sides searched for plunder—and trouble. They found it everywhere.

Union general O. M. Mitchell complained of the brutality of his men. But he himself was given to punishing civilians, sending wagonloads of filched cotton up north for personal profit, and justifying property seizures as payment for the Rebels' destruction of local bridges, trestles, and trains. In neighboring Jackson County, four civilians were arrested because Yankee pickets had been shot at several miles away.

The death of General Robert L. McCook at the hands of the Fourth Alabama Cavalry further inflamed the Yankees and led to the widespread burning of homesteads and the killing of a sick Rebel soldier home on furlough. "It became a rule to hold a community responsible for all attacks made by the Confederate soldiers," Walter Fleming wrote. The people had been "ground into the dust."

Some Rebels and civilians began to seek revenge against the Northern aggressors. "The Confederate irregular cavalry became a terror even to the loyal southern people," wrote Fleming. The hostilities grew so bitter that the taking of prisoners began to give way to on-the-spot executions. But local Union sympathizers gave as good as they got. A number of them welcomed the blue troops, supported them by ambushing Confederate forces, or joined them as members of the First Alabama Union Cavalry, further fueling the animosity.

Legitimate actions of war took place, too. In late April 1863, Colonel Abel Streight, commanding fifteen hundred Union troops astride rowdy mules, set out through the mountains south of Ider with a bold plan to cut the railroads from Chattanooga to Knoxville and Atlanta and destroy Rebel supplies in Rome, Georgia. Confederate general Nathan Bedford Forrest lit out after him. Streight passed through Gadsden, Center, and Cedar Bluff. As his mules wore out, he rustled horses. But Forrest persisted. His force of six hundred men fell upon the exhausted Yankees and beat them into surrender at Rome.

Skirmishes were continuous, though few have made the history books. But the impression of one murderous moment in time may have been left on a mountain trail near Betty's house, for it is clear something happened there.

If the place has a remarkable history, Betty's family has never heard it. Nothing seemed amiss when her parents bought the land at a back-taxes sale and built the house in the mid-1960s. As in many rural communities, the roads didn't have names or pavement then. It seemed a quiet place to raise food and family.

Betty says she has never felt scared there. But her aunt is spooked by the place.

"From the time Mother and Daddy built it, my aunt didn't like it," says Betty. "In broad daylight, she'll go in, but she will not stay by herself. She says it gives her the creeps. If Mother goes to the garden, my aunt goes to the garden. If Mother goes to the mailbox at the end of the driveway, my aunt walks with her. She won't spend the night there."

The road is paved now. Betty married and moved across the mountain. But she still wonders, thirty-five years later, what she heard one lazy summer afternoon within familiar walls.

The bonds of love between mother and son sometimes transcend death.

home is where the heart is

PISGAH, ALABAMA

The story of a soul returning to comfort a loved one in time of grief is common among people sharing tales around the kitchen table or campfire. Of all the emotions that bind a spirit to earth, the greatest of these is love.

On day in the late 1940s, Earl came down the stairs of his Pisgah, Alabama, home carrying a heavy duffel bag. He was dressed smartly for his trip to a military base in Alaska, more than four thousand miles away. His mother reached for him one last time, holding tight and bracing herself for the long separation. Earl hoisted his duffelbag back over his shoulder and, reminding his mother of the date he would return, started out. As he passed through the doorway, down the porch stairs, and out through the yard, he whistled his favorite tune. He was always whistling. It was his way.

Following a long but uneventful trip to his faraway post, Earl began his tour of duty. He never completed it. One morning, his buddies could not rouse him. He had died in his sleep.

As the weeks and months passed, most of the stunned family made peace with their grief. But Earl's mother "was just grieving herself to death," her granddaughter remembers fifty years later. "She was constantly upset and worried about Earl." She couldn't understand what had happened to him. Was it a mistake? His body had come home in a closed coffin. His mother had not seen him. She could not touch him, stroke his once-soft face while confessing her love to him in the long night during the wake. The next morning, they had lowered him into the naked earth, then gently pulled his choking mother away.

In her sorrow, Earl's mother had only his parting words to cling to—words that had made it clear not only that he *was* coming home, but even *when* he was coming home. She thought of him every day. *Maybe he'll write*, she found herself thinking. She felt secretly eager when mail time drew near each morning, even leaving the eggs frying on the stove or the laundry swinging by one pin when she heard the crunch of gravel heralding the postman's approach. She moved her chair to the window and spent more time looking down the road than she did mending or snapping beans. "Light's better here," she told the family.

The day Earl was due to return, she just didn't feel up to going to the church singing. She stayed home. That evening, she fell into bed but couldn't sleep. The grief seemed to wash over her afresh. In the middle of the night, she threw the tangled covers off and set out for the outhouse. In the light of a nearly full moon, she had no trouble picking her way across the roots and ruts of the worn path. It was too cool to bother looking for copperheads in the damp grass. She pulled the plank door open and let it close partway. The baying of dogs in the distance sounded like a dirge. Even here, perched on a cold seat, she thought of Earl. He once got stuck in the outhouse, she remembered, before they bought a real seat to cover the crude hole.

As she started back to the house, she heard whistling. Earl's tune! Clear as a fiddle, too. She stopped and steadied herself against an old dogwood. Looking up toward the house, she saw a soldier coming through the yard with a duffel bag on his back. His whistling grew louder as he neared the steps and sprang up onto the porch. It was Earl!

As he went in the front door, she ran in through the back, which allowed a view straight through to the living room in the front of the house. She saw Earl, real as rain, walk into the living room.

"I'm home," he said.

Then he vanished.

"He was always one to play tricks," remembers the granddaughter, "and Grandmother thought he had slipped upstairs or something real quick. She had every one of them out of bed, searching the house. They looked under beds, they looked in closets—anywhere he could've possibly been hiding. But after that, Grandmother thought that Earl was home. She didn't see or hear from him again, but *he was home*."

The family thought it was just her mind playing tricks. "No one else ever saw anything there. Only my grandmother saw him. But it put her mind at rest."

Years later, the old home between Flat Rock and Pisgah was torn down and its lumber salvaged to repair other houses.

But no matter to one Alabama soldier. Home is where the heart is, and his is with Mama.

graveyard time shift

HOLLYWOOD, ALABAMA

Most ghost stories involve some tragic tale of love or life gone wrong. The emotional content of such stories is easily grasped and accounts in great part for their timeless appeal. But the bizarre happenings described in this tale cannot be tied to the frailties of the human condition, for they do not seem tied to anything human at all.

Irene Hastings wears a T-shirt, a pair of sweatpants, and tennis shoes. Her dark auburn hair is simply cut, but her blue eyes glimmer with dazzling intensity. Behind those stunning eyes is a woman who divines secrets. "Reen," as her friends know her, was born with "the sight." She often sees what others miss but mostly keeps her discernments to herself. They might make her stand out, and she's not the type to cause a fuss. Besides, some of the entities she has come across have frightened her, and she's not always eager to relive the encounters. Yet her gentle reserve can be breached with patience. It's worth the effort.

Reen's story about the legendary Mud Creek Primitive Baptist Church could keep a person up at night, lights on. Still, as alarming as it is, it does not rate as the most forbidding of her experiences. But it is without question the strangest. She remains at a loss to explain it and to this day refuses to visit the church and cemetery without friends and the benefit of full daylight.

Reen learned about the church from a ghost book. "It's like a tale—if you come here and stay at midnight, walk around the church three times, and look inside, you'll see an old-timey marriage ceremony going on," she says. Reen enjoyed the story but didn't really believe in that sort of thing.

Her friend Rita agreed. She'd heard such nonsense before. "It's like the one at Bethany Baptist in Shake Rag [outside of Scottsboro]. They say if you drive around it thirteen times—"

"Yeah, thirteen times, I've done that," says Reen.

"—supposedly a hearse chases you away," continues Rita. "That's what I've read. In reality, if you go around it thirteen times, by the eleventh time, there's usually somebody chasing you out, and it's the police."

For some reason, old churches inspire the supernatural imagination. Reen's friends wanted to explore the old Mud Creek cemetery. With or without ghosts, it is a place of abiding historical interest. Founded in 1819, the church was one of a group of Primitive Baptist congregations organized by north Alabama pioneers. Its large cemetery begins almost at the church door and spreads way beyond the little white building. Over the years, the number of congregants in the graveyard began to exceed those in the pews. So far, the tombstones mark the lives of a thousand souls. Among them, no doubt, lie some who do not rest easy.

Reen's family and friends pushed her to go with them to the church one night. She shook her head. They insisted. "Come on, we'll all go in the van."

The graves at Mud Creek Primitive Baptist Church in Hollywood, Alabama, date back to the early 1800s.

Against her better judgment, Reen relented. The group pulled up to the left of the dark church and parked in the gravel lot. Reen was on the passenger's side, which faced the building. She had her window up. "There were eight of us waiting for midnight because the doorknobs are supposed to glow," she says. "We were watching that church."

Midnight came and nothing happened. "At ten after midnight," says Reen, "there was a glow coming out the door of the church, all around the door in the cracks, like when you turn the light on in the bedroom and close the door and you can see around it. That's what it looked like. They had said the doorknob started glowing. I didn't see the doorknob glow. But everything [else] was aglow. It took my breath away.

"Then there was this white, milky triangle-looking thing. I don't know if it dropped down from a tree or what. It didn't look like it come from the church." Reen felt that the entity possessed awareness—that it paused to look directly at them, sizing them up. The group members didn't want to look back at the strange apparition. They were scared. It didn't seem friendly. "It was a I'm-going-to-get-you type feeling," says Reen. "We came there to find it, and we found it!"

Abruptly, the entity raced toward them. "Everybody hit the floor of the van. It just *whoosh*ed and came through the van. It came through the fender and came right through everything. It was just that quick. It came right through me, like ice. It got me, it really did. I saw it, and I felt it. Everybody saw it. People were locking their doors."

Reen started screaming. She looked down and saw blood on her right hand. It was scratched, but her window was still up. She could hear the group screaming, "Let's go, let's go!"

"I didn't even have to tell my husband, 'Let's go,' " she says. "He was gone. We left. This place has always done me that way." Reen doesn't know why the entity chose to assault her. "I was the only one with a crucifix on," she points out.

Everyone saw it, not just Reen. So the usual explanation that psychics attract entities because they alone recognize them doesn't hold up. Regardless, Reen vowed that night to never again return to the church in the dark.

That was not the end of it, though. The cemetery seems a green and peaceful place during the day, lightly shaded by cedars and oaks. Reen found herself drawn back. She went with her husband and son Jason to check on one of the ancient trees that had been ripped and blackened by lightning. But first, to test the old fable, they decided to circle the church several times, then peek in the windows. Reen saw nothing unusual inside.

It was one of those clear fall days that makes a person feel the world is safe and ripe with possibility. Reen began to wander through the moss and stones, lost in pleasant thoughts. But she snapped out of her reverie when she realized she no longer saw her husband or Jason nearby. She was alone. The last time she'd seen them, they were behind the church. When she turned to look again, they were gone. *Why aren't they around me? Where did they go?* she wondered. *Are they planning to scare me?*

"I didn't want to walk up on those big tombstones and have them yell 'Boo!' " she recalls. "I went around the church real careful-like and said, 'Come on, guys. Quit!' " She called several times, but there was no answer. "I don't know if I was lost or they were. The van was gone. I was mad because it was my van." But she felt anxious, too, because she hadn't heard them walking in the dry leaves toward the van, or the van starting up, or the gravel crunching as it drove off. Fear wrapped its cold fingers around her.

Then Reen heard them yell. She turned and looked back toward the road. Husband and son were as relieved to see her as she was to find them. Nineteen-year-old Jason was tearful.

"They said it was about half an hour I was gone," Reen says. "They were mad at *me*."

"That's not funny," she told them. "I didn't do anything. You guys left me."

"We were all mad at each other," Reen says. "Somebody was gone for about half an hour, and I still ain't figured out who it was. And when I found them, the van was there." They told Reen they had never moved the van. So where did it go? Where did they go? Or was it Reen, after all, who had disappeared?

Mediums say the concept of linear time is irrelevant to ghosts. Some students of the paranormal theorize that ghosts are not the spirits of dead people but simply the impressions of those who slip through from the past to the present by way of a time shift.

Reen didn't see any ghosts that day, but might she have appeared as one to someone else? Could she have shifted forward a few hours, days, or months to another time? Or did the van and the men disappear instead? Reen has no idea.

"There are good Christian people buried there," she says. Yet she believes something peculiar haunts the old cemetery—an angry energy. "But I still don't believe in a lot of these go-around-the-church tales."

She won't be going around this one alone ever again.

Quick—There's a Ghost!

Reen, her best friend, Rita Strugula, and a law-enforcement officer from a nearby county, all members of the North Alabama Paranormal Research Society, took my husband and me to see the cemetery at Mud Creek Primitive Baptist Church on a bright February day. Right in front of the church, an untidy mound of red clay covered a new grave. Above the dirt, a small sign tacked to a tree instructed, "No digging in the cemetery" without permission. We thought the sign gave the unintended impression that graverobbing is a problem here.

As at most old cemeteries, the grounds are shaded and inviting. We walked around, taking pictures and talking. The officer, early in his ghost-hunting career, had carried a camera and tape recorder, but he found that they usually malfunctioned in the presence of the supernatural. Now, he carries just a compass.

Nothing strange happened. We walked toward the front to leave and stood near the cars. Just then, Reen said she saw something near the new grave. I quickly turned and snapped a photo. My fairly new Nikon is dependable, but no photo came out.

"When she said something about seeing something," says the officer, "I was holding the compass right on north, steady. The compass moved fifteen degrees." The needle had moved toward Reen and the entity.

"It will come towards me," says Reen, who knows the phenomenon well. The entity wasn't hostile. She thinks it was the woman who was recently buried. Even souls at peace are known to linger near their graves for a day or two.

We made straight for our cars and left in a whirl of dust.

The Moody Brick, built in 1855, has risen from near ashes twice.

the moody brick

KYLES, ALABAMA

If spirits of the dead cannot find peace because cruel suffering goes unnoticed and unpunished, then surely no one should be surprised to find these angry entities haunting an old plantation house. Such a place strips a person's very humanity. And if the soul cannot throw off the shackles of bitterness, bondage of the body becomes bondage of the soul.

The Moody Brick is a fine home, stately and commanding. Everyone in neighboring Scottsboro and thereabouts says so. "If you go in a coffee shop here and talk about the Moody Brick, people will tell you about it," says Reen Hastings, local medium and seeker of ghosts. "It's a nice community, but people don't like coming near this old house. They'll drive by it, but they won't stay. Strange things do happen, weird things."

Driving north on County Road 33 prepares the perceptive traveler for a glimpse into the Moody Brick's dark past. The littered road passes stumps reaching up through dark swamp water, acres of hot cotton fields, and patched, time-worn houses. The landscape has the feel of an old postcard that has been bleached out in a harsh sun.

Sometime before 1855, Carter Overton Harris likely replaced a log house with the two-story brick structure. His slaves molded the red bricks from clay down by the creek. Some say their suffering was seared into each one.

The Harris family farmed about twenty-five hundred acres. They planted a thousand acres in cotton, a crop that wearies the soil and swallows up a land's life force over the years. Broomsedge took the fields, and a wealth of dirt washed down the hillsides. The old house followed suit.

According to tradition, the brick home, like so many buildings in the path of war, served as a hospital in 1863 during the Chattanooga and Chickamauga campaigns and in 1864 when Union soldiers swarmed over the valley along the railroads. Before leaving, the Yankees filled a cemetery with their dead and torched the house for good measure. But the solid walls refused to fall to the flames.

Ownership passed to the Moody family in about 1872 through an estate sale. By then, the house was a frightful place. A visitor touring the farm in 1879 described it as "so much abused and neglected as to present an inviting retreat for ghosts and hob-goblins." Nonetheless, the three Moody brothers set out to bring life back to the farm, raising cotton, other crops, and livestock. They provided better-than-average housing for their tenants, as well as stables and gardens. The tenants were, wrote one observer, "cheerful and happy" and "warmly attached to the Moody."

In 1888, a spark from the chimney consumed the interior but left the brick walls intact. The Moodys rebuilt the home and in the next few years made some changes that resulted in a mix of architectural styles.

Then, once more, the Moody Brick fell into neglect. When the Lee family bought it in 1990, the glass was gone from every window. The Lees generously invested time, money, and hope in their new home. The results are stunning. But no one thereabouts can forget the home's past. History can't be plastered or painted over.

Standing on County Road 64 near a large maple that weeps over the front lawn, Reen Hastings admires the house. But she worries that, like earlier residents, the newest owners won't stay. "There have been several, but they don't stay. They remodel it, but then they leave. Nobody can live there."

Rumors of tragedy cling to the house like ivy. Some speak of mass murder there after the war, Reen says. "All the white inhabitants were murdered in bed by the [ex] slaves," the story goes. The slaves were caught and hanged from the large oak over the cemetery in front of the house. If the tale of wholesale murder is suspect, the story of hangings rings plausible. The Ku Klux Klan arrived in northern Alabama by 1869. So much arson, assault, and slaughter ensued that troops were called in to restore order.

To be sure, there was plenty of heartache before the Civil War, leaving slaves with good reason to bear resentment toward their overseers. "For the slaves' happiness and contentment, it was the policy of slave owners to keep them ignorant, so that the slaves may not be influenced by abolitionist's [sic] literature to escape . . . and gain their freedom," wrote early Jackson County historian John Robert Kennamer.

Not surprisingly, a patrol system was necessary to control the slaves. "If a slave was caught off of his master's premises without a written pass," wrote Kennamer, "and he was not on his way to church or to his work, he was caught and given fifteen or less lashes of the cow-hide, by the patrollers, and carried back to his master."

Life at the Moody Brick reflected the harshness of the times. Families passed down stories of slaves being chained, beaten, and even killed in the basement. Reen tells of someone who explored the basement and took one of the iron rings to which slaves were tied. So much bad luck befell her that she returned it.

But it seems neighbors would not have spoken well of the Harris family if they had abused their slaves. Perhaps they or their hired overseers are accused unjustly these many years hence. The heavy rings may remain from the years when the basement served as a kitchen, and the barred windows could speak of the days when Yankees stowed Confederate prisoners in the belly of the Moody Brick. Soldiers from both sides sleep forever in the plantation's red clay.

Apart from the five graveyards on the place—two of which are lost—body parts are buried there from Civil War hospital days. Also lost is the knowledge of who lies buried within an unmarked, sealed rock enclosure in the family cemetery. Some speculate it is the household slaves, still trapped by plantation walls in death, as in life. That is not likely. Slaves were usually buried in unmarked or crudely marked graves. Nonetheless, the occupants of those walled-in graves, whoever they are, may not rest easily. And they aren't the only ones.

Local residents whisper about unexplained deaths and baffling suicides. A maid named Sally Ann, they say, took her own life by jumping off the front balcony. "A lot of times, you'll drive by at night and see Sally Ann standing on the balcony. You can see her in the door a lot of times," Reen says. She does not know what drove Sally Ann to leap to her death.

Reen has heard talk of five killings in four years. "One of the last carpenters that worked in here was halfway in the door, dead," someone told her. Another carpenter, rumors say, committed suicide at the Moody Brick. Others tell of the builder who murdered his wife and stuffed her inside the stout walls. Her angry ghost has been seen roaming the halls late at night. A less hostile specter is that of a teenage girl named Elizabeth. "You can go by and see her standing there [in the window]," Reen says. "Her doll is still in the window. It's so sad."

There are witness to the strange goings-on. "An older woman who lives [around] here sometimes says that her son hears things and sees things moving in the house," says Reen. "But she thinks he's crazy." Reen does not agree. "I felt a lot of bad stuff here. Every time I come up here, it just gives me the creeps."

Fear of the house goes back many decades. One visitor remembers staying there as a child of six or seven. Despite the home's beauty, she had heard so many ghost stories about the old place she felt safer sleeping with the covers over her head.

Judi Weaver, director of the Jackson County Heritage Center, says she knows of no mysterious deaths there, at least not in recent years. She says the Moody Brick remains an exquisite treasure and doesn't think for a minute that ghosts roam its spacious rooms. But it's natural, she says, for people to believe the home is haunted, considering all the years it stood abandoned and forlorn.

Modern teenagers have been drawn to the Moody Brick out of curiosity or in response to dares. Three boys once entered the vacant house at night armed only with flashlights. One boy's foot went through the rotted staircase. Someone took his arm and pulled him up. Turning to find who had helped him, the boy saw no one. He was alone. The other two boys were elsewhere in the house. Other teens vandalized the empty home, perhaps as a way to cover their fear of it. The family graveyard was also vandalized. Or so Reen thought.

"One of the weirdest things happened," she says. "My husband, my son, and I and a friend who's a radiologist at a local hospital went into that cemetery. We were mad because stones were toppled over." She thought teenagers had done it.

"Some were crumbled. They were cracked. We came back the next day—we were going to try to do something about it—and it was like nothing was ever wrong with them." All the stones were solid. Reen and the others began to wonder if they had even been there the day before.

Judi Weaver warns against exploring the cemetery in the summer. But it's not ghosts she fears. Rattlesnakes slither among its rocks and tombstones, their mood made worse by the heat.

Rita Strugula, who has investigated hauntings for more than a decade, says the Moody Brick is exceptional. "You don't know what's going to happen, but you can pretty much guarantee *something* will happen," she says. "It is one of the most active [sites]."

The house is a mother lode for supernatural photography. Rita frequently finds that a mist appears in developed photos. She has captured shots of bricks that seem to be falling out when they're clearly well anchored. She has photographed people—a man walking in from the field and a man in an upstairs doorway—who, she insists, were not there when she snapped the shots. One evening, she captured images of fairies fluttering over the lawn. She says the Moody Brick is the last

Lens flare may be the cause of the strange mists often seen in photos of the Moody Brick.

place in the world she would expect to see such beings and has no idea what their presence portends.

Rita feels lucky to have captured anything. Equipment trouble is common on the site.

Reen agrees. "My cell phone never works here," she says.

Rita tells of a person whose camcorder, loaded with new batteries, refused to tape during her entire visit. When Rita later looked at her own pictures of the camcorder operator, the woman held a human head instead of her camcorder.

The Moody Brick still seeks to reclaim its former grandeur and take its place once more as a Jackson County landmark. But there remains an empty look about it, as if no one has ever lived there at all. After the passage of countless souls through its rooms and halls, the home still feels as if it has no soul, no color, no blood.

But as everyone in Jackson County knows, it will rise again.

murder in alabama

North Alabama

Imagine you're in your house and people begin to arrive uninvited in the middle of the night. They look at you, talk about you—commenting you look pretty awful—and make plans concerning you. But they never say a word to you or ask what you'd like or what you think. Worse, you're falsely accused of burglary. Wouldn't you be angry? Ghosts are people, too.

"I don't even remember the first murder scene I saw," says Deputy Sheriff James Garrett—not his real name. "That's how many I've done." But the deputy will never forget one murder investigation.

It was barely Saturday. The sharp sliver of moon had already slipped away, and a February chill deepened over north Alabama. Deputy Garrett was investigating a suspicious situation in the county's northwestern corner when the dispatcher radioed at 2:19 A.M. with instructions to report to the scene of a shooting in a small community on the other end of the county, about fifty miles away. A 911 caller had told the dispatcher someone had broken into his home. He shot the burglar, he confessed, and figured the person was dead.

Deputy Garrett knew the caller and his common-law wife well. He had been to their mobile home many times on domestic violence calls. The couple had been together for some time, closely bound by strong ties of anger.

"I'd arrest her," Garrett says. "She was a tough lady. I've had to scuffle with her."

His relationship with the suspect was almost amiable. "He's a nice guy. I've known him for years."

But testimony that later came out during the trial showed the suspect had made a habit of assaulting the victim. And she had dished it out, too—cutting, stabbing, flinging hot grease, and threatening to blow up his truck.

The deputy, accompanied by a rookie and a detective—his cousin—arrived on the scene at three o'clock in the morning. The caller was still there, on the phone with the dispatcher. Garrett directed the dispatcher to tell the caller they had arrived and to instruct him to put the gun where the officers could see it and then move away from it when they came to the door. The caller complied.

Garrett found it wasn't a burglary after all. "The guy's live-in girlfriend had been shot. He was intoxicated and thought if he made it look like a burglary, it'd be excused and he wouldn't be charged."

The man told the deputy, "I know you can't be shooting folks outside, so I let her get in the house."

"Billy, you can't be shooting people no way," Garrett said.

"She broke in."

"She lives here. You can't break in where you live."

The victim lay sprawled on the floor in front of the sofa. Garrett quickly determined she had been dead for fifteen or twenty minutes. The lower side of her face was missing, parts of it splattered on the ceiling. "From the nature of the wound, I don't think she died instantly," he says. "Blood loss was probably the cause of death." But he does believe that, mercifully, she was unconscious before death.

"The rookie guy came in, and he almost got sick. He was about twenty-four, and this was his first murder scene." Garrett sent him outside to handle less gruesome tasks. Another detective came and took the suspect away.

Deputy Garrett called the Alabama Bureau of Investigation—standard procedure for a major crime. The one ABI agent available was in Jackson County, two hours away.

While they waited, Garrett and the detective began their investigation. They found evidence the man had washed his hands of the murder before calling 911. The bathroom towels were bloodstained, but the telephone was clean. "I collected everything out of the trash can with blood on it," Garrett says. "We did our photography. After a time of evidence collection, there is only so much you can do."

He had already met with family members who gathered outside. They had heard the news, told Garrett what funeral home they wanted to use, and, after some coaxing, left.

"We had done our part of the investigation . . . everything except bag the gun." But the officers couldn't leave. They had to secure the scene until the ABI agent showed up.

"I don't know about you, but I don't want to sit here and look at a dead body for the next two hours," Garrett told his cousin.

The men went into the kitchen. "We set there so we wouldn't have to look at her, to be honest with you," he recalls.

They had nothing to do but talk. Deputy Garrett has never been known to be at a loss for words. "I don't know what we were talking about—football, just things we talk about."

The house was quiet. The windows and doors were closed tight against the cold. In the living room, a small table lamp spread a dreary blanket of light over the silenced woman.

Nearby, a wall heater glowed faintly. The atmosphere was like the still, heavy air before a tornado strikes. Their training had not prepared the two men for the quick shift that was about to conjure a storm out of the calm.

"There was a little shelf hanging on the wall over the couch, right above where she was laying. I call it a girly shelf," Garrett says. "It had little dolls, little porcelain stuff. All of a sudden, all the stuff on that shelf just came off. It reminded me of somebody just taking their hand and raking it off. When it hit, it covered where she was laying and hit in the floor and on her and around her and in her blood. Some of it was glass. None of it broke. It was a carpeted floor, so it just scattered. I looked over at my cousin, and he looked at me. We tried to ignore it. I've known him all my life. I could tell there were things starting to run through his mind."

Neither man gave voice to his dread. They remained seated but wary.

A few feet away, a small stack of unused flat, square paper bags used to collect evidence lay on the counter. The men had not tagged and bagged the murder weapon yet. They had placed the twelve-gauge shotgun atop the stack of bags, thinking the ABI agent would want to inspect it first.

One of the bags began folding itself over the long gun. "It kinda wrapped like somebody took their hand and ran across it," Garrett says. "The bag actually lifted up. We saw it." They heard the sound of paper crackling.

Deputy Garrett looked at his cousin. "Hey, man, I don't think she knows she's dead."

"One more thing like that, and she's going to be dead by herself because we're waiting in the car!" Garrett's cousin said.

The dead woman must have preferred company. Nothing else happened, says Garrett. The ABI agent arrived, and the two men left.

"I believe her spirit was still there," Garrett says. "I think she was angry because she knew what had happened. She was lashing out. She focused her anger on something that was definitely hers. I've been in law enforcement for ten years, and I can't begin to tell you how many murders and suicides I've worked. That's the only time I've ever had anything like that.

"I never was a big believer in ghosts. . . . My mom's very religious, and that goes against everything that we were taught. You died, you were going to heaven or somewhere else, or you're waiting on Judgment Day. You're not wandering around earth."

He does believe now.

The suspect was released on bond and lived in the trailer for many months after the shooting before being convicted of murder. Deputy Garrett hasn't heard a thing from him. Or her. If the victim is still there and still angry, the man may look forward to a few quiet years away in prison.

THE MAKING OF A TRAINED OBSERVER

James Garrett brings exceptional credibility to his story. As an Alabama county deputy and a police officer for a small town, he is a trained observer. He became a law-enforcement officer in the mid-1990s and soon thereafter went through the state-trooper academy in Selma. "From the very start at the academy, you're trained to pay attention to detail."

Officers are required to get twenty-four hours of training each year, but Garrett seeks out more when he can. In 2004, he voluntarily completed many times that number. But no amount of training can take the place of experience in the world of law enforcement. After years on the force, Garrett can stay cool under circumstances that would unnerve most people, making him an unusually reliable witness in unpredictable and sometimes terrifying circumstances.

He was born to wear the badge. "I can't see myself doing anything else."

"John A. Murrell—The Headless Outlaw"

Coates, Robert M. *The Outlaw Years: The History of the Land Pirates of the Natchez Trace.* New York: Macaulay Company, 1930.

Coulter, Curtis, "John A. Murrell's Hidden Gold." In *Down Country Roads: Stories of Sale Creek, Tennessee.* Self-published, 1990.

Dyer, J. Pope. "The Last Days of John A. Murrell." *Chattanooga Sunday Times* magazine section, June 28, 1936.

Excerpt about John A. Murrell from *Independent Gazette*, November 14, 1823. Bledsoe County Library vertical file.

Garrett, Jill L., compiler. *Obituaries from Tennessee Newspapers.* 1980. Reprint, Southern Historical Press, 1995.

Higgins, Randall. "Outlaw Legend Thrives." *Chattanooga Times*, June 24, 1980.

Howard, H. R. *The Life and Adventures of John A. Murrell, the Great Western Land Pirate.* Philadelphia: T. B. Peterson and Brothers, 1845.

Leftwich, Nina. *Two hundred years at Muscle Shoals: being an authentic history of Colbert County, 1700-1900; with special emphasis on the stirring events of the early times.* Tuscumbia, AL: c. 1935.

Morgan, Marshall. "Sharp-Eyed, Hymn-Singing, Bible-Quoting Murderer." Bledsoe County Library vertical file.

"Murrell, Colorful Outlaw, Died Here before Civil War." *Bledsonian Banner*, August 9, 1945.

"Notorious As a Highwayman." Bledsoe County Library vertical file.

Penick, James Lal, Jr. *The Great Western Land Pirate: John A. Murrell in Legend and History.* Columbia: University of Missouri Press, 1981.

Phares, Ross. *The Reverend Devil.* New Orleans, LA: Pelican Publishing, 1941.

Robnett, Elizabeth Parham. *Bledsoe County, Tennessee: A History.* Signal Mountain, TN: Mountain Press, 1993.

Sheperd, Judge Lewis. "John A. Murrell, a Forgotten Desperado." *Chattanooga Times*, March 17, 1912.

"The Story of John Murrell, Outlaw." *Bledsonian Banner*, August 16, 1945.

Wellman, Paul I. *Spawn of Evil.* Garden City, NY: Doubleday & Company, 1964.

Williams, Emma Inman. *Historic Madison: The Story of Jackson and Madison County, Tennessee.* 3rd ed. Jackson-Madison County Homecoming Steering Committee, 1986.

"Shadow Man"

"Paranormal Phenomena: Shadow People." *About.com* (2006). http://paranormal.about.com/library/weekly/aa022502a.htm (accessed 2006).

"The Pitty Pat"

Coulter, Curtis. *Down Country Roads: Stories of Sale Creek, Tennessee.* Self-published, 1990.

"The Tears of Little Nina"

"Beloved Lady Dies, Victim in Path of Auto." *Cleveland Daily Banner*, September 7, 1928.

"The Blood Stained Mausoleum." *Ghosts & Spirits of Tennessee* (2002-5). http://johnnorrisbrown.com/paranormal-tn/mausoleum (accessed 2005).

Bowers, Larry C. "The Legend of Nina Craigmiles." *Cleveland Daily Banner*, October 31, 2003.

Coultry, Andy. "Clement Hall in ETSU update." *Linda Linn's Kentucky Home and Ghost Stories: Stories from Kentucky and Tennessee* (2001-6). http://members.tripod.com/~lindaluelinn/index-9.html (accessed 2005).

"Craigmiles Tomb Considered Mysterious Landmark in City." *Cleveland Daily Banner*, November 1, 1955.

Cummings, Frank, and Katharine L. Trewhitt. *History of St. Luke's Episcopal Church, Cleveland, Tennessee, 1867-1967.* Cleveland, TN: 1967.

"Mrs. Craigmiles' Residence." *Cleveland Journal*, December 27, 1900.

"The RMS *Titanic*, Cargo Manifest." *ThinkQuest*. http://library.Thinkquest.org/21583/cargo.htm (accessed 2006).

Russell, Randy, and Janet Barnett. "The Weeping Mausoleum." In *The Granny Curse and Other Ghosts and Legends from East Tennessee*. Winston-Salem, NC: John F. Blair, Publisher, 1999.

Snell, William R. "Cleveland had its ghosts in the late 1800s." Article from *Cleveland Daily Banner* in Cleveland Public Library vertical file.

Snell, William R., ed. *Bradley County Ghosts & Other Haunts*. Cleveland, TN: Bradley County Historical Society, 1998.

Trewhitt, Katharine L. "Mausoleum has sparked several superstitions." Article dated October 15, 1986, in Cleveland Public Library vertical file.

"True Ghost Stories: Blood Stains on the Mausoleum." *Bradley News Weekly*, October 22-28, 1997.

"A GHOST GETS REVENGE"

"Carlson's Ghost Seen by Simons." *Chattanooga Daily Times*, October 12, 1919.

"Lost Records in Old Murder Come to Light." *Chattanooga Times*, October 26, 1926.

"Ridge Has a Mystery." *Chattanooga Daily Times*, July 31, 1919.

"The Spiraling Trap"

"Finishing Touches Being Put on Lock and Dam at Hale's Bar—Power on in Few Weeks." *Chattanooga News*, September 13, 1913.

Livingood, James W. *A History of Hamilton County, Tennessee*. Memphis: Memphis State University Press, 1981.

Mooney, James. "63. Ûñtsaiyi, the Gambler" (from *Myths of the Cherokee*). *Internet Sacred Text Archive* (2001). http://www.sacred-texts.com/nam/cher/motc/motc063.htm (accessed October 3, 2005).

Parker, Barry. "Happy Bunch Greets Sara." *Chattanooga News-Free Press*, December 23, 1974.

———. "Prepare to Lift Sunken Towboat." *Chattanooga News-Free Press*, November 10, 1974.

Raulston, J. Leonard, and James W. Livingood. *Sequatchie: A Story of the Southern Cumberlands*. Knoxville: University of Tennessee Press, 1974.

"Tugboat Sinks in Tennessee River with 34,000 Gallons of Diesel Fuel." *Chattanooga Times*, September 4, 1973.

"Mary Greene of the *Delta Queen*"

Fermi, Stefano. "*Delta Queen*: A national historic landmark preserves America's past." *Tutto Crociere: The Cyberspace Cruise Magazine* (1998). http://www.cybercruises.com/deltaqueen.htm (accessed July 29, 2005).

Rayser, Dr. V. Fred. "Ghosts of the Mississippi River" (from *Fate Magazine*). *Llewellyn: New Worlds of Mind and Spirit* (October 1, 2001). http://www.llewellyn.com/archive/fate/49/ (accessed July 27, 2005).

"The River People: Captain Mary Becker Greene." *National Mississippi River Museum & Aquarium* (2005). http://www.mississippirivermuseum.com/fame/greene.cfm (accessed July 29, 2005).

"THE CURIOUS CASE OF GENERAL GRANT'S HEADQUARTERS"

Armstrong, Zella. "Ghostly Sentries Believed to Walk in House Where Gen. Grant Maintained His Headquarters." *Chattanooga News*, October 13, 1933.

———. *History of Hamilton County and Chattanooga, Tennessee*. Vol. 2. 1931. Reprint, Johnson City, TN: Overmountain Press, 1993.

———. "Old Grant House a Landmark." *Chattanooga Times* magazine, March 1, 1936.

Birchmore, W. E. *Chickamauga and Chattanooga National Military Park: A Historic Monograph*. Chattanooga, TN: 1895.

"General Grant's Ravaged Headquarters Here Ordered Razed by BHA." *Chattanooga Times*, February 13, 1966.

"Grant Home to Become Chapel." *Chattanooga Free Press*, May 22, 1969.

Grant, Ulysses S. *Personal Memoirs of U. S . Grant*. Vol. 1. New York: Charles L. Webster and Company, 1885.

Gregory, Hamilton. "Grant's War Headquarters Here 'Forgotten Relic.' " *Chattanooga News-Free Press*, August 10, 1961.

Hopkins, G. M. *Atlas of the City of Chattanooga, Tennessee.* Philadelphia, PA: 1889.

Loop, Sue Mills. "When U. S. Grant Lived Here." *Chattanooga Times* magazine, June 12, 1932.

"READ HOUSE REVENANTS"

Armstrong, Zella. *History of Hamilton County and Chattanooga, Tennessee.* Vol. 1. 1931. Reprint, Johnson City, TN: Overmountain Press, 1993.

"Colorful Early History Recalled by Opening of Read House; Crutchfield House, Scene of Many Stirring Incidents, Was among Most Famous Hostelries South of Mason and Dixon's Line." *Chattanooga Times*, July 26, 1926.

Govan, Gilbert E., and James W. Livingood. *The Chattanooga Country, 1540-1976.* 3rd ed. Knoxville: University of Tennessee Press, 1977.

"The Historic Read House." Handout, The Read House Hotel.

"Planned Extension of Read House to Cost $1,000,000." *Chattanooga Times*, October 21, 1923.

"The Read House Hotel." Handout, The Read House Hotel.

Schneider, Fred G. "Read House Is Purchased by Noe Chain." *Chattanooga Times*, June 30, 1943.

Shearer, John. "Employees Tell of Ghostly Incidents: Read House Has Room with a Boo." *Chattanooga Free Press*, October 27, 1996.

Wiltse, Henry M. "The Crutchfield House in the Days of Old." *Chattanooga Times*, August 4, 1918.

"Haunted Hooper Hall"

Combs, Craig. "Echo Staff Braves Night in Haunted Hooper-Race." *University Echo*, November 4, 1993.

———. "Phantom Folklore Haunts Hallowed Halls of University." *University Echo*, October 22, 1992.

"John C. Hockings Takes Own Life." *Chattanooga Times*, January 8, 1924.

Pendleton, Michele. "School Spirit Haunts Hooper-Race Hall." *Echo*, November 2, 1984.

"Timely Topics." *University Echo*, January 18, 1924.

"Little Margie"

Denton, Lisa. "Where Do Local Ghosts Hang Out?" *Chattanooga Times*, October 30, 1996.

"Night Drummers"

Armstrong, Zella. *History of Hamilton County and Chattanooga, Tennessee*. Vol. 2. 1931. Reprint, Johnson City, TN: Overmountain Press, 1993.

"Battle of Lookout Mountain, November 24, 1863, Hamilton County, Tennessee." In *Chattanooga Area Civil War Sites Assessment*. Chattanooga, TN: Chattanooga-Hamilton County Regional Planning Agency, 1998.

Cozzens, Peter. *The Shipwreck of Their Hopes*. Urbana and Chicago: University of Illinois Press, 1994.

Dana, Charles A. *Recollections of the Civil War*. New York: D. Appleton and Company, 1902.

Fullerton, Joseph S. "The Army of the Cumberland at Chattanooga" (from *Battles and Leaders of the Civil War*, vol. 3). *The Western Theater in the Civil War: Army of the Cumberland*. http://www.aotc.net/Chattanooga.htm#Fullerton (accessed 2005).

Korn, Jerry. "Decision on Missionary Ridge." In *The Fight for Chattanooga*. Alexandria, VA: Time-Life Books, 1989.

"TN-17 Actions on Lookout Mountain, September-November 1863." In *Chattanooga Area Civil War Sites Assessment*. Chattanooga, TN: Chattanooga-Hamilton County Regional Planning Agency, 1998.

Wilson, John. *Lookout: The Story of an Amazing Mountain*. Chattanooga, TN: Roy McDonald, Publisher, 1977.

"BLADES AND ROSES"

Obituary of Captain Hemen W. Grant. *Chattanooga Daily Times*, May 28, 1912.

Obituary of Leila Wert. *Chattanooga News-Free Press*, September 14, 1987.

Wilson. *Lookout: The Story of an Amazing Mountain.*

"Green Eyes Searching in the Night"

Bohannon, Keith S. "Battle of Chickamauga." *The New Georgia Encyclopedia* (September 5, 2002). http://www.georgiaencyclopedia.org/nge/Article.jsp?path=/HistoryArchaeology/CivilWarandReconstruction/Events-8&id=h-642 (accessed September 22, 2005).

Cummings, Kevin. "Area residents, former park official report seeing eerie spectre" (from the *Catoosa County News*, October 31, 2003). *Catt.com.* http://www.catt.com/article.php?story=20031031151742448 (accessed 2005).

Evans, E. Raymond. *Chickamauga—Civil War Impact on an Area: Tsikamagi, Crawfish Springs, Snow Hill, and Chickamauga.* Walker County, GA: City of Chickamauga, 2002.

Gordon, General John B. *Reminiscences of the Civil War.* New York: Charles Scribner's Sons, 1903.

Robertson, William Glenn, et al. "Staff Ride Handbook for the Battle of Chickamauga, 18-20 September 1863." http://purl.access.gpo.gov/GPO/LPS59172 (accessed 2006).

Sartain, James Alfred. *History of Walker County, Georgia.* Dalton, GA: A. J. Showalter Company, 1932.

"Fifes and Drums"

Dolan, Charlou, with annotations by V. S. Schoolcraft. "Georgia Source Book: Snodgrass Family." http://freepages.family.rootsweb.com/~clansnodgrass/ga.html (accessed October 1, 2005).

Lusk, Charles W. "Few Survivors of Civil War Days Still Live in Vicinity of Chickamauga Battlefield." *Chattanooga News*, September 22, 1923.

"Dead Boys Walking"

Korn, Jerry. *The Fight for Chattanooga*. Alexandria, VA: Time-Life Books, 1989.

"Miss Clarissa's Angry Yankee"

Evans. *Chickamauga —Civil War Impact on an Area*.

"GA-5 Actions, skirmishes, and engagements around Lee and Gordon's Mill, September 6-20, 1863." *Chattanooga Area Civil War Sites Assessment*. Chattanooga, TN: Chattanooga-Hamilton County Regional Planning Agency, 1998.

Tsikamagi Garden Club. *Chickamauga Yesteryear*. Chickamauga, GA: Chickamauga Business Center, 1998.

"Little House of Spirits"

Mooney, James. *Myths of the Cherokee*. 1900. Reprint, New York: Johnson Reprint Corp., 1970.

Simek, Jan F. "Prehistoric Use of Caves." *The Tennessee Encyclopedia of History and Culture* (2002). http://tennesseeencyclopedia.net/imagegallery.php?EntryID=P048 (accessed in 2005).

Varner, Gary R. "Caves, Rocks & Mountains: Portals to the Otherworld" (from *Menhirs, Dolmen and Circles of Stone: The Folklore and Magic of Sacred Stone*). *Authorsden.com* (September 10, 2005). http://authorsden.com/visit/viewarticle.asp?authorID=1215&id=13264 (accessed in 2005).

"THE HAUNTED DOORWAY"

Glass, Patrice Hobbs. "The Boom Towns of McLemore's Cove, Georgia: Kensington and Estelle." Master's thesis, Middle Tennessee State University, 1999.

————. "The Chattanooga Southern Railway Company and McLemore's Cove." *Chattanooga Regional Historical Journal* 2 (July 1999), 135-49.

"It's a Magic Town." *Chattanooga Daily Times*, June 21, 1890.

"The McLemore Cove Town Full of Push and Enterprise." *Chattanooga Daily Times*, June 20, 1890.

Walker County, Georgia, Heritage: 1833-1983. LaFayette, GA: Walker County History Committee and Walker County Historical Society, 1992.

"THE GENERAL'S ROCKER"

Bean, David J. "Gen. Hood unlucky in battle, unlucky in love." *Washington Times*, October 7, 2000.

Chesnut, Mary Boykin. *A Diary from Dixie*. Edited by Ben Ames Williams. Cambridge, MA: Harvard University Press, 1980.

Foster, Samuel T. *One of Cleburne's Command: The Civil War Reminiscences and Diary of Capt. Samuel T. Foster, Granbury's Texas Brigade, CSA.* Edited by Norman D. Brown. Austin: University of Texas Press, 1980.

"Wagon Train"

Fleming, Walter L. *Civil War and Reconstruction in Alabama.* New York: Columbia University Press, 1905.

The Heritage of DeKalb County, Alabama. Clanton, AL: Heritage Publishing Consultants, 1998.

The Heritage of Jackson County, Alabama. Clanton, AL: Heritage Publishing Consultants, 1998.

Partain, Rich. "Streight's Raid." *Welcome to Cullman County, Alabama.* http://www.co.cullman.al.us/history2.htm (accessed in 2006).

Sayers, Alethea D. "Raid of the 'Mule Brigade': April 11-May 3, 1863." *Civil War Web.com* (1999). http://www.civilwarweb.com/articles/12-99/streight.htm (accessed in 2006).

"Graveyard Time Shift"

The Heritage of Jackson County, Alabama.

Remington, Craig W., ed. "Cemetery Locations by County." In *Historical Atlas of Alabama.* Vol. 2. Tuscaloosa: University of Alabama, 1999.

"The Moody Brick"

Brown, Chasity. "Moody Brick legend lives on." *Daily Sentinel* (Scottsboro), April 26, 1998.

Chambless, Ann, ed. "The Moody Brick." *Jackson County Chronicles*, July 1995.

Grider, Randy. "Old Moody homeplace is a reminder of days gone by." *Daily Sentinel* (Scottsboro), July 17, 1990.

"History of Moody Brick and Its People." Scottsboro Public Library vertical file.

Kennamer, John Robert. *History of Jackson County*. Winchester, TN: Southern Printing and Publishing, 1935.

"North Alabama Paranormal Research Society Presents Real Ghost Photos: Pixies." *North Alabama Paranormal Research Society* (2003-5). http://www.naprs.us/Pixies.htm.

"The Moody Brick Historical Landmark," on file in the Jackson County Heritage Center, c. 1986.